GRAVE MISTAKE

A Spencer Funeral Home
Niagara Cozy Mystery

Book 3

Janice J. Richardson
CANADA

~ Books by Janice J. Richardson ~

The Making of a Funeral Director (non-fiction)

A Spencer Funeral Niagara Cozy Mystery series

Casket Cache
Winter's Mourning
Grave Mistake
First Call

* Amazon * Kobo * Nook * iBooks *
* Chapters/Indigo *

ACKNOWLEDGMENTS

Writing is solitary work. When the beta readers, cover designer and an editor join in, then it becomes teamwork. The joy is truly in the journey, shared.

Once again, thank you team Brian, Pam, Morgan, Jennifer G. and M.J.

1

Elaine, the funeral home administrator, passed the first call of the day to Marcia, who just happened to be readily available. Puzzled by the expression on the usually unflappable Elaine's face, Marcia looked at her quizzically as she took the handset. Elaine mouthed the word 'later' and left Marcia alone in the office.

When she completed the call, Marcia stayed at Elaine's desk inputting the information into the computer, before going to Jennifer's small office off the lounge to update her. She found Elaine and Jennifer deep in conversation. There wasn't room for the three of them, so Marcia stood at the door.

"The Larson family will be in shortly to make arrangements. Do you want me to see them?"

Jennifer looked up from her computer screen as she and Elaine exchanged glances.

"What? Is there something wrong?" Marcia looked from one to the other.

"The Larson family has a history of problems

around town. I was just filling Jennifer in on some of their antics," Elaine said.

Jennifer interrupted her office manager before she could continue and addressed Marcia.

"It's your decision. The last few days have been exhausting. You worked hard."

"So did you," Marcia reminded her best friend.

"Here it is." Jennifer glanced back at her computer screen. Peter had completed inputting all the previous call records on the computer before he left for college, cutting the search time down to seconds. "This is their first visit here."

"It could be a challenging call," Elaine said.

"Or not," said Jennifer, sounding upbeat. "Depends on who shows up. We are obligated to serve them."

"Although, my recollections of them are from years ago, so anything could have happened in that time," Elaine said.

"Am I missing something here? What challenge? I spoke with Alymer Larson, he was a nice man. His father died of natural causes—nothing out of the ordinary. I don't mind taking the call Jen."

Another phone call interrupted their discussion, and the conversation about *why* the Larson's were a challenge was set aside. Marcia didn't get another chance to speak with Elaine, who left to run errands.

Less than twenty minutes later, two men and two women, all middle-aged, entered the funeral home donning grim expressions. As she met them at the door, Marcia noted their body language and demeanor. It would help her determine how best to make the family comfortable—something they did not resemble in the least.

"I'm Marcia."

One of the men shook her hand briefly. "I'm Aylmer, this is Elmer." He pointed to the man beside him. The other two are Alma and Elma." He fluttered his hand in the direction of the two women. She did her best to keep her face neutral, trying not to react to the odd far-too-similar names. She did raise an eyebrow as she led the group to the office. *That must have been the challenge Elaine wanted to discuss.*

"I'm sorry to hear about your father's death." She took a seat behind the desk once everyone was settled, but didn't get a chance to continue.

"I'd like to—"

But Aylmer interrupted her and took over, "Yeah, well, that's life. We want cremation." He didn't look at his siblings when he made his rather blunt statement. Marcia was a little taken aback at

3

his seeming indifference.

Alma turned to her brother, her gaze shooting daggers. "No, we want burial, not cremation. He should be beside Mom."

Marcia's heart sank. The Larson's had been in the funeral home barely two minutes and it was obvious this family was not happy in one another's company. Elma had not stopped scowling since she arrived, Elmer had his arms crossed—his lips pressed into a thin line, and Alma had rolled her eyes several times.

Aylmer pushed out his chest and puffed up like a frigate bird at his sister's statement about burial. It was as if he tried to be the alpha male and take up all the space in the room. The siblings' names could have been a clue—with the Larson parents giving their children names that sounded the same, perhaps as a result, each sibling had felt the need to fight for their individuality. Marcia jumped in.

"Did your father have a preference? Did he discuss his wishes with you? Put anything in his will?"

"We didn't talk about it," a rather timid-looking Elma stated.

"No," Elmer agreed.

Hoping to prevent further discord, Marcia

4

turned to Elmer and Alma. "What do you think your father would have wanted?"

"Cremation," Aylmer stated.

"Burial," Elma shot back. Elma had quickly lost her timidity. She sat up straight and leaned over to Aylmer, daring him to challenge her. The four of them started talking at once, each one defending their position on their father's disposition.

"You're not the boss."

"You never paid attention to him."

"He wanted to be buried beside Mom."

"So, he could be cremated, then buried."

"No one in the family has been cremated. What makes you think dad wanted cremation?"

Marcia didn't get the sense that any one of the siblings were grieving. It felt to her that a few minutes into the arrangement, they'd stopped trying to keep their anger in check—that any attempt at social norms had given way. She could feel their suppressed rage. The four of them were like an overstretched elastic about to snap. She needed to intervene.

"Perhaps you could compromise," Marcia stated loudly over the cacophony. Four pairs of eyes, all unfriendly, looked at her. Undeterred, she continued, "Do you plan to have visitation?"

"Yes," Elma said.

"Not necessary," Elmer countered.

"What do you mean, not necessary?" Alma snapped. "Of course we will have visitation. Our friends want to pay their respects."

"What friends?" Elmer snarled, releasing his folded arms and throwing his hands up in the air. He snorted. "You have friends? I don't think so."

"Visitation, cremation, burial in the family plot?" suggested Marcia, hoping to diffuse the situation by ignoring him.

Aylmer sat back in his chair, pouting. The siblings did agree on a minister. She helped them write the obituary for the paper, then contacted the minister, who agreed to do the service in the chapel at the funeral home.

One more hurdle to go. "I would now like to take you into the selection room so you can choose a casket for your father." The four siblings, uncommonly silent, trailed behind. But less than a minute later the harsh discord started again.

"You are the only one who thinks Dad wanted cremation. You're wrong, as usual."

"All you want to do is spend money," Aylmer growled. Then the four of them started talking at the same time, squabbling over the choice of casket.

It was at that point Jennifer came into the selection room. Marcia caught her gaze and gave a slow blink, a signal to each other that support was needed. They seldom used that signal, but Marcia was glad to have it as Jennifer responded in kind and joined Marcia in her role as referee, listening to what each sibling wanted.

Alma and Elma wanted an oak casket, in keeping with their father's love of wood carving. Aylmer and Elmer wanted a cloth-covered particleboard, in keeping with their penny-pinching ways, as Alma not so graciously pointed out in a comment about her "cheapskate brothers".

In spite of the confusion and squabbling, Marcia managed to negotiate a compromise—an ash casket. Neither funeral director cared about what the casket cost, selling caskets was not their favourite part of the job. A casket, however, was a necessity.

Once the arrangements were complete and the door shut behind the family, Marcia plunked herself in a club chair in the lounge, slid down slightly and let out a whoosh of air. The silence was a relief as Jennifer made tea for both of them and joined her. They didn't speak for a few minutes, each lost in their own emotional analysis about the dysfunction they'd just witnessed.

"I think we're going to need a security firm to ride herd during visitation and the funeral," Marcia said.

"How bad could it be? They're stressed, they just lost their father, maybe things will settle down." But even Marcia didn't believe the note of hopefulness in her friend's voice.

"The atmosphere in the office crackled with tension. I could *feel* it before they opened their mouths. Once they started bickering I had to use my 'outside' voice." Marcia reached for her tea and took a sip. "Really Jen, it's like a cartoon. What kind of parents give their children the same name?"

"With different spellings," Jennifer added lamely. "It's hard to believe they were even allowed to do that, you would think a social service agency or the government would intervene. It's just cruel."

Elaine, who had returned from running errands, entered the lounge to find the two funeral directors sitting in their favourite chairs, staring into space, each reliving the disbelief in their moments with the Larsons, their tea all but forgotten beside them.

"Hi, girls. How did the arrangements go with the family?" she asked as she prepared a coffee.

Both funeral directors looked at their office manager wordlessly. Elaine looked from one to the

8

other as she poured cream into her coffee. "Not good?"

"Not really," Marcia said. "They are one unhappy group of siblings. There's no love lost between them."

Elaine put the cream back into the fridge and took a seat kitty-corner to them. "I know a little bit about the family, I had started to fill Jennifer in earlier. You see, I went to school with one of the girls. Alma, or was it Elma?" She paused, frowning in concentration, then shook her head. "Anyway, it doesn't matter. Their father, Albert, had been a shoe store owner, growing his single shop into a chain of stores. When he retired, he turned the stores over to his sons, who ran them into the ground." She put her cup down. Jennifer and Marcia hung onto every word.

"Over time, one by one, the stores closed, until even the flagship store was forced to shut down. Each son blamed the other for the failure of the business. I've heard over the years that the Larson family had problems. Even the girls fought a fair bit among themselves."

"Is that what you were trying to tell us earlier before we were interrupted?" Marcia asked.

Elaine nodded, making a "sorry, I tried" kind of

face.

"Great," Marcia's voice dripped sarcasm. "We'll need referee shirts."

Elaine's smile was a little weak. "I doubt that would do much good. My husband used to coach for the kids' hockey teams. Two of the children were on opposite teams. Both sets of parents ended up on the ice and started brawling over the referee's call. Needless to say, the kids were dismissed from their teams and the parents were charged."

"That should be a lesson," Jennifer said, trying to sound positive.

"It wasn't. There are more than a few places in the area that won't allow some members of the family on their property, including the mall."

"That bad?" Marcia asked.

"Yep, that bad." Elaine looked at them sympathetically. "I didn't want to say too much about the family because, well, as I mentioned they are older now and I would have thought they'd have settled down."

"Then after what we saw this morning, I'll take your advice Marcia, and hire a security guard for visitation," Jennifer said. "That should be a deterrent. I'll also phone Brent and see if they have any previous Larson family funerals on record."

***

By the end of the day, Jennifer and Marcia had completed the transfer and casketed the Larson patriarch. The obituary was in the paper and family flowers had arrived, a simple casket spray. It was the first time in over a week that Jennifer was able to say goodnight to her staff and shut down Spencer's at 5:00 p.m.

She went back to her office and called Brent, her manager at Williams Funeral Home. Once they caught up on what his family was up to and how many calls he had, he put her on hold to check the records on the Larson family.

He was back in a few minutes.

"Good news or bad news first?"

Her heart sank. "Good news." He chuckled. "Sorry, it's not funny. As I scan through the file there actually appears to be no good news, other than the fact that there is a file. It shows that Mrs. Eleanor Larson died fourteen years ago. A note here says the family had been asked not to return after an incident." Jennifer could hear him flipping pages.

"Uh oh. That sounds ominous."

"There's an old bill here for damages. It numbers into the hundreds of dollars. No record of payment."

"Thanks, Brent."

That was all Jennifer needed. She immediately hired a security guard for the next evening's visitation. Grief expressed through anger was not uncommon and she did not want the funeral home to be the recipient of angry, destructive behaviour. She was even more determined to prevent an injury to other family members or staff. At the very least, she wanted to believe their behaviour was grief but had a sinking feeling Marcia was correct, it was pathologically more.

The next evening as various members of the family trickled in, Jennifer noted a distinct absence of older people. The four Larson siblings were dressed in subdued colours, each one arriving separately.

Elma and Alma looked as if they'd been to the same hairdresser, sporting old-fashioned pin curls. Aylmer and Elmer wore dated suits, their thinning hair combed over the shiny spots on the top of their heads. Aylmer and Elma arrived at approximately the same time and did a double take when they spotted the security guard. Marcia, hoping to distract them, quickly greeted them both by name and led them to the suite. Less than a minute later they returned, striding purposefully down the corridor to the lobby.

Jennifer stood near the door, opening it for the younger family members who were in and out and had gathered under the portico to smoke and talk. The presence of the security guard did not seem to bother them in the slightest, nor did it settle them down. They were loud and boisterous, laughing with their friends. They were not dressed in suits like their parents, and it soon became clear that the *friends* Alma had suggested would be attending the visitation were just the friends of the younger generation. The growing crowd of noisy young people made Jennifer uneasy. So did Elma as she marched over.

"Why is there a security guard sitting there?" Elma griped like an angry parent, startling Jennifer as she came up behind her.

Jennifer had suspected there might be such an inquiry from one or more of the Larsons. The security guard stuck out like a sore thumb. She turned slowly to face the glowering Elma. Aylmer quickly closed the gap behind his sister.

"Protection," Jennifer responded politely.

"For whom?"

"For you, your family, the funeral home." She almost felt guilty over the lie about protection for the

Larson family. It was all about her funeral home.

"Well, I'm deeply offended." Jennifer tried to ignore Aylmer's scowl. "You might have let us know. We would have gone to another funeral home. It's insulting. I'll be reporting you to whatever Board governs your business and the Better Business Bureau."

As if to reinforce his threat, Aylmer stepped closer to Jennifer, a little too close for comfort, his massive frame dwarfing hers. She did her best to stand tall against his bullying behaviour. Outwardly she remained all business, freezing her face into neutral. Inwardly she was mush. *Please, please, please find another funeral home,* said the voice in her head. At six feet he towered over her five-feet-two-inch frame. She felt cornered with no way to get around him.

"If there is no damage, then I will cover the cost of the security guard. I am not prepared to ask the security guard to leave. If you wish, you may transfer to another funeral home. I would be happy to facilitate it for you." She fought to keep her voice from quivering. He was starting to frighten her.

The sharp scent of alcohol lingered on his breath, assaulting her senses. Alcohol and anger. It reminded her of her father's struggle. *As if grief and*

14

anger weren't enough.

"How dare you threaten me," he growled and moved in closer, backing her up against the wall.

Jennifer felt her courage drain. She hated confrontation. The Larson family were not the ones being threatened. Marcia immediately moved up beside her. The security guard stood up and moved in a bit as well. Having Marcia there was comforting.

"I'm sorry you feel that way, Mr. Larson. Apparently, there have been a few incidents in the past that involve your family. It is not a threat, its insurance." Marcia's voice held firm.

"You'll be hearing from my lawyers. How dare you! Who do you think you're talking to? There will be repercussions." By now he was bellowing and Jennifer was sure he could be heard all the way across the road. She chose not to respond to that question, it would have been a double-bind, no-win answer.

The air crackled with tension as Marcia and Jennifer silently stood their ground. Elma made the first move, tugging at Aylmer's sleeve as his face flushed a darker shade of red. "Come, we can deal with this later."

As he followed his sister back to the suite,

Jennifer and Marcia exhaled slowly. The security guard sat down again, shaking his head.

"Whew, I thought he was going to hit me." Jennifer could feel the tension leave her body as she relaxed.

"Me too."

"I know this family. I've had dealings with them in the past," the guard said. "Our firm has a long list of incidents involving the Larsons. The younger ones can be pretty rowdy."

"So can the older ones," muttered Marcia under her breath. She turned to Jennifer. "I should have mentioned this sooner. Ryan told me last night that some of the Larson's were well-known to the police." Ryan was Marcia's boyfriend, a Detective Sergeant with the Niagara Regional Police.

"After we locked up last night I spent a few hours researching court records and the newspapers in the region. There's been a lot of violence in the family. One has to wonder if it is genetic."

Marcia looked at her incredulously. "That's how you spent your evening? Reading court records and old newspaper articles?"

"Well, yes," Jennifer inadvertently sounded a little hurt. She folded her hands in front of her, feeling very small. "I needed to know what to expect."

Marcia was quick to apologize as she picked up on her friend's body language. "I'm sorry, I wasn't trying to be mean. I try to put work behind me when I leave."

"No, don't apologize. Now that I own two funeral homes, work is a constant. I don't mind. Grimsby and I sort of watched TV at the same time. I was in my apartment relaxing. I had my laptop."

"Ryan and I were curled up watching a movie."

"As you should be," Jennifer responded quickly. She didn't want Marcia feeling sorry for her. Jennifer was happy with her life and work. Before Marcia could reply, a crash from the lounge interrupted the conversation.

With the security guard behind them, she and Marcia rushed to the entrance to the lounge. One glance was enough for the security guard, he pulled his phone and dialed 911.

"Don't go in," he ordered.

Neither funeral director had any intention of getting close to the escalating brawl unfolding before them. Marcia stood at the door watching with fascination as the adult children of the Larson siblings erupted into a full-contact altercation.

By the time the police pulled into the parking lot

four minutes later, broken dishes were strewn on the floor, chairs were tipped over, and it seemed everyone was yelling and punching and no one was listening. Jennifer watched in horror as one young man threw a healthy punch, slamming his victim against the wall, leaving a hole. She was even more taken aback when another young man took a swig from a flask before taking a swing at the person closest to him. Some of the girls who were hanging out with the brawlers made a beeline for the front door, squealing like baby pigs. It reminded her of a bar room fight from an old western movie. Unfortunately, John Wayne didn't show up to stop it.

By the time the dust cleared, it required three squad cars and six officers to settle the worst of them down. The police took six to jail and booked them in for the night. Several were taken to hospital for sutures.

Even as the police did their best to settle the brawlers, Jennifer overheard an escalating argument from the suite about whose child was and whose wasn't at fault. One of the officers went to the suite to intervene.

A drunken Aylmer tossed the casket spray, then tipped over several chairs as Elma and Alma, who were screeching insults at him, ran for cover as a second officer showed himself. They continued to scream obscenities at their brother as they were escorted down the hall. Marcia came up beside Jennifer, her only comment almost made her smile.

"You can't make a silk purse out of a sow's ear."

Clearly dressing up did not improve one's behaviour. Jennifer stood at the door and surveyed the scene. The flowers lay on the carpet surrounded by dark splotches of water with pieces of flower oasis scattered across the rug. The lamp that had been hurled at one of the sisters by Aylmer had smashed to pieces. He had single-handedly trashed the suite, ranting and raging. Elmer was missing in action, he'd fled the funeral home at the first sign of trouble.

The only consolation was that the casket containing Mr. Larson was still upright on the bier. Aylmer was quickly apprehended, handcuffed and put into the back of a squad car. He continued yelling obscenities back at his sisters as the vehicle pulled away. Elmer watched from his car until the police left, then exited the parking lot, tires squealing. The tail lights of his Toyota faded in the distance as a dejected Jennifer stood watching.

The police and security guard ushered the rest of

the family out the door, and Jennifer locked it behind them, shaking with a mix of anger and fear. Leaning up against the wall and breathing deeply, she attempted to calm down even as her anger boiled. Alcohol had been smuggled in, her funeral home trashed.

Waiting until the last car left the parking lot, Jennifer and Marcia surveyed the destruction. While insurance would cover the furniture replacement and repairs, it would not alleviate their disgust at the situation. After documenting the damage with photos, the two of them gloved and gowned, cleaned up the blood splatter, and removed the broken furniture and smashed cups in the lounge before cleaning up the suite.

It took two hours out of an already too-long day. The security guard had reassured them that his report would be available should they require it. As Marcia left for the night, the two them agreed that the Larson visitation was the strangest they had ever witnessed.

2

The next morning, not a single person showed up for the funeral. Jennifer called Aylmer, then Elmer. Both calls went to voicemail, so she left a message. A curious Marcia was eavesdropping. Alma did answer her phone.

"Just bury him," was the curt response to the question about the funeral service. "We're done with your funeral home." She abruptly disconnected.

Jennifer turned to Marcia. "Should we give the minister the option of proceeding with no mourners or send him on his way?

"It's my family, guess I should ask. Maybe he'll do the graveside for us. I don't want to plunk Mr. Larson in the grave without some kind of service. There's no dignity in that."

The minister was only too happy to accept the honorarium and get back to his day, declining to do the service. He'd made it clear he'd had enough of the Larson family when he visited them to discuss the service. Jennifer and Marcia could hardly blame him.

"It's hazard pay," Marcia said after the minister left, her voice tinged with sarcasm. "It was good of him to try to help."

The graveside service was to be held at Whispering Pines, a small cemetery at the edge of town. The manager, Doug, had the opposite personality to Mr. Whitney, the manager at the large city cemetery. He was kind and considerate and Elaine had assured them he would assist them once they reached the graveside. Jennifer called Jeff at Williams Funeral Home to help them get the casket to the grave, making it the four people she required. Jeff was to follow them in the van to the cemetery and he arrived at the funeral home in less than ten minutes.

Between the three of them and with Elaine's help, they put Mr. Larson into the funeral coach. Dark clouds boiled in the sky. Jennifer had checked the weather early that morning, the forecast called for rain with possible thunderstorms—a rather dreary late November day, and unseasonably warm for November.

"Let's motor," said Marcia as she scanned the sky. "I don't want to be anywhere near a cemetery in a thunderstorm."

Jeff looked at her, surprised. "Scared? *You're* scared of a cemetery?"

"It's not the cemetery I'm afraid of, it's the lightening. Rain and umbrellas with trees around or even open spaces don't mix. More than one funeral party has been injured by lightning. Jennifer and I did a corner's call where a cemetery worker was killed by a lightning strike. The accompanying storm was miles away. One can't be too careful."

"I suppose not," said Jeff thoughtfully. "Now you have me on edge."

With Jeff following the funeral coach, Marcia drove to the cemetery.

"Think the rain will hold off?" Jennifer asked.

"Probably not."

Indeed, as they drove through the cemetery gates a few drops splattered the windshield.

"Go, go, go," Marcia said, as she accelerated. "Let's hustle. We may have to do our committal service from the coach."

"We won't melt in the rain. But if I even hear a hint of thunder or a see a flicker of lightning, I'm heading for cover," Jennifer said.

Pulling up to the designated section they did not see a cemetery vehicle or staff. There wasn't time to hunt the manager down. They'd come early, so they would stop by the small office as they left to notify him to close the grave. Jennifer's rule about four on a casket was tossed aside in order to expedite the burial before the rain hit.

Moving quickly, the three of them lugged the casket to the grave, and with no dignity, plunked it on the lowering device. As the wind picked up, a significant crack of thunder made Marcia squeal. She ran for the funeral coach, Jennifer and Jeff right on her heels, the committal service forgotten. The clouds rolled faster as gusts of wind almost knocked them sideways. Jeff ran ahead of them to the van and disappeared inside. The sky was increasingly ominous and getting darker as the storm grew. The air smelled like sulfur and had a yellowish tint to it.

"That sounded like an explosion," panted Marcia as she started the funeral coach. "It wasn't a rumble or a growl, it was a nuclear event." The rain had picked up as large drops hammered the windshield.

Simultaneously, both their cell phones alerted. Jennifer pulled her phone out of her pocket. "Tornado watch, we should take cover."

She dialed Jeff to see if he was aware of the danger.

"Yeah. I got the alert too."

"Let's get to Williams Funeral Home, it's the closest. I'll watch the sky and stay on the phone with you. If we see anything, we'll pull over and run for shelter. My main concern is getting out of the cemetery, it's too open around here."

Marcia was already speeding for the gate, Jeff close behind. As the wind picked up and the rain and hail pounded the vehicle, Jennifer couldn't see ten feet in front of them. The coach shook with each blast of the wind and the sound, coupled with the pounding hail, it made them feel isolated, as if they were trapped in a tunnel. She could see hints of Jeff's headlights behind them. Her skin prickled with fear.

As the darkness increased, and the wind shrieked, Jennifer saw the fear etch onto Marcia's face. She wasn't feeling safe either. If there was a tornado near them or upon them, they had no way of knowing. By now the air was electric, almost crackling.

"Are you there, Jeff?"

"Yes," was his curt response. "This is getting weird."

"We're almost there. It'll be all right," Jennifer reassured, although she wasn't convinced, her heart felt like it was going to pound out of her chest. A deafening crash of thunder followed by a lightening flash that made the hair on her arms stand up, made them both scream. The noise of the storm increased to a roar. It sounded like a freight train closing in.

Pulling up to the back door at Williams, both drivers parked as close to the door as they could and made a beeline inside. In the few seconds it took to exit the vehicles and enter the funeral home, they were drenched. They panted more with fear than exertion, as they stood inside the door, relief written all over their faces.

"You OK?" Jennifer asked Jeff. His face, drained of colour, betrayed his fear. His eyes were wide and his freckles looked like someone had dotted them on with a pen.

"I think so." He looked from Marcia to Jennifer and back again. "To be honest, no. I have never seen or felt anything like that before."

"I did once, when I was about twelve," Jennifer said. "A small tornado brushed the edge of town. The hail was huge. The wind took all the leaves off a few trees on our property and blew away part of the fence. We had to run to the basement. I have a healthy respect for any kind of weather watch/warning now. Looks like we may be here for a while, let's go downstairs and have coffee."

Desta, upon hearing their voices, met them at the top of the stairs. "That's quite the storm. Is everyone OK?"

"Just fine, thanks." Marcia replied as she pointed over her shoulder. "But those two look like drowned rats," she announced as they started down the stairs to the lounge.

"And you don't?" Jeff countered. Marcia grinned. She liked pushing his buttons. Jeff prided himself on his appearance, always carrying a comb with him. The gentle bantering lowered the tension they'd felt in the storm. He grinned back at her.

"Tea or coffee?" Jeff asked.

"Tea, please. I am going to find Brent, be right back," Jennifer said over her shoulder. She could hear Marcia and Jeff continue to tease each other.

Brent was at his desk, staring at the computer screen. She stood in the doorway and waited until he looked up, her damp clothing making her uncomfortable.

"What brings you here?" Jennifer could see that his usually pleasant expression had been replaced with concern. His mouth was tight and straight, and he had a tiny frown.

"The storm hit fast, we got a tornado warning.

27

Williams was closer so we detoured here from the cemetery."

"I was just following the weather too. There was a tornado sighting in town. Hope the school got the kids to safety." The words were barely out of his mouth as the power flickered, then with a whoosh, went out. The emergency lighting clicked on a few seconds later.

Jennifer sensed his fear. "Can you reach the school?"

"I've been trying. Cell phone service is spotty." Brent picked up his cell and dialed. He pulled the phone away from his ear and frowned. "No service." He picked up the landline. "Line's busy."

Jennifer heard him inhale deeply, his anxiety growing about safety of his family. Doing her best to ease his fear, she immediately regretted her next statement. "The wind picked up when we were at the cemetery, it's wicked out there but I'm sure the school is on top of it."

Fortunately, he didn't answer; he didn't seem hear her. He redialed the number for his children's school and listened intently, his frown slowly easing. She watched his shoulders visibly relax.

"The message says the children are safe, and they will keep them at the school until after the storm. Then the parents can come pick them up." He hung up, sat back in his chair and exhaled with relief. His face was calmer as he looked up at her.

"Power may be out for a while. The coffee is hot for now, let's sit for a bit until the storm settles." Brent rose and followed Jennifer downstairs to join Desta, Marcia and Jeff, who were discussing the storm.

At the bottom of the stairs, Jennifer pulled out her cell phone and dialed Spencer's. It rang several times, then the call dropped. Alarmed, she excused herself, put her phone in her pocket and ran back upstairs to the landline.

"Be right back," she said over her shoulder. "I have to check on Elaine."

In the front office, she pulled back the curtains to look outside. The storm appeared to be subsiding, she could now see across the street. Small branches were strewn on the road, what was left of the fall leaves had been stripped from the trees. Relieved to see the storm abating, she dropped the drape and picked up the landline.

Elaine answered on the first ring.

"Are you all right?" Jennifer couldn't keep the concern from her voice.

"I'm fine. What about you and Marcia? My

husband said there was a small tornado near the cemetery. I couldn't reach you."

Jennifer's relief at hearing Elaine's voice was palpable. She sank into a chair.

"We made it back to Williams a few minutes ago. Why don't you close up for the day, I'll be along eventually. I doubt much will be happening with the power out and the streets needing cleanup."

"Thanks, I might do that. My husband offered to pick me up. I'm so relieved to hear that the three of you are OK."

"We'll talk tomorrow. Thanks, Elaine."

Heading back downstairs, Jennifer picked up the tea Jeff had made her and sat down.

"Elaine is fine. I'm sending her home for the rest of the day. There was a tornado near or at the cemetery apparently, not much more information yet. Let's hope there was no injuries or deaths. No point working without power. Brent, the storm seems to have eased up. Go get your kids and go home. I'll cover the phones. You too Desta. Jeff."

Brent rose immediately, washed his cup and turned to his boss.

"I'll be available if you need me."

"Go," she responded with a wan smile. Truth was, if there were deaths as a result of the storm, they could be working around the clock for several days. Brent knew that, so did Marcia, but they were not prepared to acknowledge or discuss it yet. Jeff and Desta said their goodbyes and disappeared upstairs.

Jennifer glanced over at Marcia, who'd become uncharacteristically quiet. In fact, her friend looked a little pale.

"Marcia?"

Marcia looked up at Jennifer and grimaced. "I think something I ate disagreed with me." She held her body stiffly, as if she was afraid to move. "That coffee didn't help."

Jennifer waited until Brent and the rest of the staff left and the door closed behind them before answering, "You're not OK, are you?"

Marcia shook her head. "No, I'm not. I was uncomfortable when I got up this morning, now I'm queasy and my right side hurts." Her breathing was shallow. Marcia wasn't a complainer.

"What would you like to do?"

"Ryan's probably busy." She put her hand on her side and grunted. "I want to lie down."

"Should I take you home?"

"I don't think I should drive. Can we go to your place?"

31

"Let me help you upstairs, then I'll shut down the funeral home. I'll come get you when I'm done."

Carefully Marcia got to her feet. Jennifer stood beside her, ready to assist. Marcia walked to the stairs slowly, hunched over like an old person, her breath coming in short gasps. Reaching the bottom of the stairs she looked up, then turned to Jennifer.

"I'm not sure I can do this."

"Try using the railing on the left side, I'll support you on the right."

Marcia complied, grunting with pain on the slow ascent. Upon reaching the top of the stairs, Jennifer lowered her into a nearby chair.

"Do you think you should go to the hospital?"

"No," said Marcia, half panting, half grunting. "If people were injured in the storm, the Emergency Department will be full. I'd rather wait and see if this settles."

"OK. She didn't argue with Marcia or try to change her mind. It wasn't her decision to make, unless Marcia took a turn for the worse.

"I'll be right back." Jennifer shut off all the light switches except for a few small lamps. When the power came back the funeral home would look as it always did.

She went out the back door to the coach and

drove it to the front of the funeral home. Leaving it running, she went in to get Marcia.

"Can you walk to the coach?"

Marcia nodded. As she stood up she inhaled sharply with pain and hunched over. She looked over at Jennifer, her face awash with misery.

"Gallbladder. It must be. My mom had gallstones. Took her six weeks to recover from the surgery."

"Was that before laparoscopic surgery?" asked Jennifer. She was becoming more concerned as Marcia got worse. She did her best to sound upbeat.

"Yeah. She had to wait about two months for surgery. If this is any indication of what she went through I don't know how she did it."

Carefully and as gently as possible, Jennifer helped Marcia into the vehicle, then locked up William's funeral home. Back in the coach, Marcia sat quietly, her eyes closed, her breathing shallow and rapid. Tree limbs and debris were scattered on the sidewalks and the street. A silent Marcia, usually ever curious and engaged, didn't even notice.

Detouring a few times because large branches blocked the street, Jennifer was relieved to finally pull into the funeral home. It was also dark in that part of town. The entire city must have been affected by the power failure. She barely glanced at the branches and debris from the storm scattered around the lot. It could wait. Right now, Marcia was her number one priority.

3

Jennifer unlocked the door to Spencer's, noting with satisfaction that the emergency lighting was working. The sky was dark and still, no more boiling clouds and wind. The rain had eased.

She poked head back into the car. "Where would you like to go? Do you want to lie down in one of the suites?"

Marcia opened her eyes and looked at her miserably. "I can try lying down. I should be near the washroom. I'm really nauseous."

Jennifer helped her out of the car and into the funeral home, easing her carefully onto the couch in the suite closest to the washroom. She ran upstairs to her apartment, gathered the pillow from the spare bedroom, a blanket from the closet and said a quick hi to Grimsby, who had stood up on his spot on the back of the couch to greet her. Grimsby meowed loudly, upset by the storm.

"I'll be back buddy." He looked at her, his eyes wide, as she closed the door and hurried back downstairs.

Marcia barely noticed as Jennifer helped her remove her jacket, put the pillow on the couch and eased her down. She let out a cry of pain as Jennifer lifted her feet.

"Are you sure you don't want to go to Emerg?"

Marcia carefully shook her head no, even that simple movement seemed to exacerbate her pain. Jennifer reached over and checked her friend's pulse. Marcia's skin was cool to the touch and while her pulse was a little fast, it was not racing.

She went to the washroom and brought back the small garbage pail, placing on the floor near Marcia's head.

Marcia was oblivious.

Quietly Jennifer sat in a chair near her, and checked her phone, turning off the volume and putting it on vibrate so it wouldn't disturb her friend.

Cellphone service was back up and Jennifer sent a quick text to Detective Sergeant Ryan Gillespie to let him know what had happened. She looked up the wait times at the Emergency Department—six hours. Jennifer knew that would depend on triage and Marcia. If she continued to have an acute problem, they'd see her immediately.

Within a couple of minutes of texting Ryan, he

responded with "on my way."

A moan from Marcia caused Jennifer to look up just as her friend's eyes flew open. Jennifer jumped to her feet and grabbed the garbage pail as Marcia started vomiting. While Marcia emptied her stomach contents, Jennifer did her best to breathe through her nose but started to retch, too. Poor Marcia didn't notice, she was too ill. Spent finally, she lay back on the pillow with a groan.

"I'll be right back," Jennifer said quietly as she took the pail to the washroom and wet a paper towel to wipe Marcia's face. She returned to find Marcia sitting up, her feet on the floor, shivering. Jennifer gently wiped her friend's face and tucked the blanket around her.

"Ryan's on his way."

Marcia showed a spark of interest at the mention of his name. "Thanks," she responded weakly.

The suite was quiet as the minutes ticked by. Jennifer sent Jeff a text asking him if he'd be available to accompany her to the cemetery to check on the casket. He did not respond.

"I think I need to go to the hospital."

"I agree. Shall I call an ambulance?"

"No," Marcia said. Jennifer realized that she'd asked Marcia about an ambulance at least twice.

While the conversation was becoming circular, Marcia probably did not remember she'd refused an ambulance at all, her pain all-consuming

"Let's wait for Ryan," Marcia said with barely a whisper, as if even talking hurt. A low rumble of thunder coincided with another bout of vomiting. Again, Jennifer did her best to control her retching as she held the pail. She had never been good with illness.

It was with a guilty sense of relief she heard the front door open. She felt herself relax at the sight of Ryan as she met him in the hallway.

"Hi Ryan, she is in the front suite." He walked briskly past her.

"Hi babe," she heard him say. She reached the door of the suite to see him smoothing back Marcia's hair. "Are you ready to go to the hospital?"

Marcia nodded, her face pale and etched with pain. Ryan, to Jennifer's surprise, scooped Marcia effortlessly up into his arms and walked to the front door. Jennifer scrambled to catch up. She opened the door to let them out, then opened the front door of his car. The wind had started to pick up again and thunder rumbled in the distance.

"Thanks," said Ryan as he settled Marcia gently onto the seat, then scrambled around the back of his vehicle to the driver's seat. He drove off.

Looking at the boiling clouds, Jennifer exhaled. She hadn't said a word to Marcia or betrayed her concern, but she *was* worried. Unable to reach the cemetery, she needed to know if Mr. Larson's casket was still sitting on the grave. Jeff had not answered her texts either, she wanted to take him with her. She didn't want to bother Brent, he needed to be with his family.

If the casket is still there, I'll call the cemetery manager. Hopefully, he was able to close the grave and I won't have to try to find help to bring Mr. Larson back to the funeral home. After locking the door behind her, Jennifer drove the twenty minutes to the cemetery as quickly as she could.

The heavy rain had starting again, blasts of wind attempted to push the van off the road. Leaves and small branches swirled in the microbursts around her. Arriving at the cemetery, she once again noticed the absence of a vehicle. The office was dark, the power still out.

Pulling up to the graveside she did not see the casket sitting on the lowering device. Perhaps the cemetery manager had lowered it. Then why was the lowering device still there? She exited her vehicle, her heart pounding. Running to the graveside she looked down. The lowering device was askew, the bottom of the grave had several inches of water in it.

Horrified, she looked around wildly. Tree branches and leaves littered the usually tidy little cemetery. A few gravestones lay on their side. There was no sign of Mr. Larson's casket. Worst case scenarios flashed through her head. Had the tornado snatched up the casket? Had it been stolen? It had been almost five hours since they'd fled the cemetery ahead of the tornado. A small tractor with a forklift on the front was parked outside a shed, the door banging in the wind.

"No. No. NO!" she yelled into the rain, her panic rising. As the storm crashed around her, she hurried around the periphery of the cemetery looking for the casket, or the remains of a casket. What if the tornado had snatched it? What became of Mr. Larson?

A distant rumble of thunder followed by a flash of lightning made her flee to the van before she completed her circuit. For the second time that day, she was soaked to the skin, the water dripping from her wet hair mixing with the tears running down her face as she scrambled into the driver's seat.

I should have rechecked the weather. We should have waited. I ought to have known better. The tyranny of the 'oughts' got the better of her and she

41

wept with fear and frustration. Drenched, chilled and frightened, she drove to the cemetery office and, ignoring the deluge of rain again, pounded on the door. No one came, there was no one there to come. She turned back to the van, dejected and discouraged and more than a little panicky. Could she lose her funeral director's license? Or worse, the funeral home license? Would it be considered misconduct if the tornado had taken Mr. Larson away? Would it be a violation of the Act? Would there be a hearing?

Sitting in her vehicle, she tried the cemetery manager again. He was the single employee, part-time staff assisted him when necessary. There was no answer. Once again, the call went to voicemail. The cemetery office line was not on answering service.

Defeated and scared, she drove home, almost oblivious to the flashes of lightening and booming thunder around her. She pulled up to the garage, parked the van inside, and locked the doors to the vehicle and the garage. Dejected, she climbed the dark stairs to her apartment soaked through and shivering. Grimsby meowed loudly when she opened the door to the apartment.

"I'm so sorry Grimsby. Let's get you some dinner." She added a couple of treats to his food, put his dish down and then trudged into her bedroom to remove her wet clothing and change into her pyjamas. Grimsby, full and feeling safe with his mistress, wound himself in and out of her legs, tripping her. Impatient, she bit her tongue. It wasn't his fault.

Unable to make tea, she opened the fridge, pulled out a can of club soda and scooped Grimsby into her arms, burying her head in his soft fur. His purrs, soothing and safe, gave her respite from the events of the day, if only for a few minutes. She fell asleep on the couch and woke to sunshine, the power restored.

Checking her phone quickly, she read Ryan's early morning text. Marcia had acute cholecystitis, a gallstone was blocking the bile duct, so she'd been admitted for pending surgery later in the day. There was nothing, not a word, from the cemetery manager. Jennifer knew that finding out what happened to Mr. Larson had to be her first priority.

4

As soon as she opened the funeral home the next morning, Jennifer logged in and checked the news. There were reports of minor injuries from the tornado, which had touched down at the edge of town. Several buildings had been levelled by the storm. It was obvious from the reports and map that the cemetery had been in its path. She heard Elaine come in and rose to meet her in the lounge, pouring her a coffee.

"Thank goodness there were no deaths or serious injuries." Elaine sat in her new favourite chair. Her favourite one had been smashed in the fiasco with the Larson family. Elaine had moved the furniture around to fill in the gaps. "Indeed, it could have been much worse."

"Marcia is in the hospital." Elaine's reaction, the shock on her face, made Jennifer realize she'd delivered that bit of news a little too bluntly. "It's OK, at least sort of. She had a gallbladder attack. They are considering surgery later today." Jennifer scrambled to make up for her poor etiquette.

"Oh no! Poor Marcia. Oh dear." One look at Elaine's stricken face confirmed Jennifer had not delivered the news well at all. "I'll get a gift basket off to her right away. She loves bath products. I'll order it and pick it up later and drop it off. I'll stop at Williams and get them to sign the card."

"As usual, you are thinking about the staff. That should have been my first priority." Jennifer sighed. "I have a few other problems to deal with today, not the least of which is a missing Mr. Larson."

"What? How can he be missing? I don't understand."

"Neither do I." As Jennifer told Elaine the story, she could see the woman's increasing concern and her heart sank. She finished with her worries about misconduct.

"Oh, my goodness, what a horrible situation. The storm was an act of God. It happened so fast, I don't think the Board would hold that against you. When did you get the alert?"

"At the cemetery, after we placed the casket on the grave. We were waiting for the cemetery manager, we were early." She looked at Elaine, mirroring the concern on her office manager's face.

"We should have stayed and put the casket back

into the coach." The dread she'd felt the day before threatened to overwhelm her again. "We were not aware of the weather watch. By the time the alert about the storm warning came through, the tornado hit."

"What did the cemetery manager have to say?"

"That's part of the problem, I can't reach him. I've tried numerous times. I'll keep calling until I get him though. With the power outage, I couldn't leave a message. I did call earlier this morning, but the answering machine didn't kick in. And he's not answering his cell phone." Jennifer kept biting her lip, unable to contain her worry.

"I don't know what to do, Elaine. Maybe I can run over again later, see if he is at the office. What if the tornado snatched the casket? It was on the lowering device, might it have caused an updraft when the tornado went through?"

Elaine shook her head. "I have no idea what you should do, except to say you have all your bases covered, so to speak. Document times and calls, just in case."

"Good plan. I'll do that. I'm just sick about this." The two of them sat in silence for a few minutes, muddling over Mr. Larson's disappearance. Then Jennifer's heart leapt and she gasped. "I have to tell the family. No, I can't. How would I word it? Your father is missing? The casket is gone? A tornado took him? They'll sue me and I'll lose the funeral home." Jennifer covered her face with her hands. "It's a horrible mess."

"I don't think they'll sue you—or can't. It's an act of God. Wait a bit until you know for sure what happened to Mr. Larson. You also have to get the repairs done in the lounge and suite," added Elaine.

"Can you recommend a good firm?" Jennifer responded absently, her mind still on the many consequences of Mr. Larson's disappearance.

"I do my own decorating, but I have gone into Design A on Main Street. They have some interesting products and pictures of the renovations and rooms they've done."

Jennifer put her cup down and leaned forward, sliding the Larson family into the back of her mind for the moment.

"I was thinking of expanding my little office off the lounge. With Peter here occasionally and Marcia full-time, I think having workstations for them might be a good idea. The selection room is large and with virtual selection available now, I don't need to carry such a big offering of caskets. We can set up a computer and go digital."

Elaine looked at her thoughtfully. "That sounds like a good plan. When it's busy here we're stepping all over each other in the front office."

"I was also thinking about renovating the apartment a bit. I'd like to screen in the deck and change the kitchen."

"Sounds like you've been mulling this over for a while. I like it," Elaine said emphatically. "You don't draw a salary. You should, you know."

"I don't need a salary. I have the apartment and a company car, and my phone is covered under the business. Other than personal stuff, such as groceries, I really don't need much at all. I'm quite happy."

"Your uncle and aunt were happy upstairs too. The apartment reflects their taste. Maybe it is time to make it your own."

Jennifer looked at her, thinking about everything that could be done to change the funeral home and apartment and nodded. "I'll check out Design A." She rose and washed her mug. Elaine downed the last of her coffee and got up too. Jennifer took Elaine's mug from her and rinsed it.

"I'll make the arrangements for a basket for Marcia."

"If I scoot out to the cemetery, I could pick up a card for her on the way back and then stop at

Williams. I should be back in a little over an hour, would that fit your plans for the day?" Jennifer asked.

"Sure, go ahead. Since Marcia may be in surgery at any point today, she'll likely not even notice I am there, poor girl."

Jennifer put on her jacket and left immediately, hoping someone, anyone, would be at the cemetery.

The roads had been cleared, making the drive easier, but when she arrived the office was still shut tight. No cars, no one. Her heart sank. This was getting serious. She went back to the car and wrote a note to the manager, noting the time and date, asking him to contact her as soon as he was available.

As an extra check, she drove by the grave again. Nothing had changed. The askew lowering device was still in place, the little tractor parked by the open shed. Something was very wrong. She felt the need to talk to Brent and get his advice.

Stopping at the mall to get a card for Marcia took a bit longer than she'd planned. Jennifer wanted the right card, and there were so many to choose from. She finally settled on a slightly sarcastic funny card.

As she entered Williams funeral home a short while later, Desta rose to greet her.

"Hi Jennifer, how's your day going?" she asked

pleasantly.

"Not too bad," she lied. It would be easy to be negative with the loss of Mr. Larson and Marcia's illness, but she understood she couldn't allow herself the luxury of projecting that negativity onto her staff.

"Marcia had to go to the hospital last night with a gallbladder attack. She may be having surgery today. I have a card for the staff to sign."

"That's awful, poor Marcia. Jeff is heading off to do a transfer, let me get him to sign the card before he leaves. I'll be back in a couple of minutes."

"Is Brent in?"

"In his office. We have a family coming in shortly."

"Thanks, Desta. I'll be with Brent." Desta was already disappearing down the hall to find Jeff.

Jennifer tapped lightly on the door to Brent's office.

"It's open."

Jennifer entered quietly. Brent's windowless office was neat and tidy. The glow from his banker's lamp gave the dark wood wainscoting a warm feel. He was entering the file information for the new call, hunting and pecking on the keyboard.

"Hi Brent, how's your family doing after

yesterday's events?"

"The kids and dogs and Julie are fine thanks. No damage to the house or property. We played games by candlelight last night and the kids are at school today."

"I know you have a family coming in shortly, but do you have a few minutes?"

"Of course."

"Couple of things." Jennifer leaned against the back of one of the chairs facing his desk. "I think it's time we hire another director here. You need more time off. I know we have an apprentice coming in about six months, but you've been busy."

He looked at her and smiled. "I've been working on that and was going to let you know I have several candidates lined up. I'll set up some interviews. Hopefully, we can both find a mutual time to meet with them."

"It might have to wait until Marcia has recovered. She is in the hospital."

Brent raised an eyebrow and cocked his head.

"Gallbladder. Acute. She became sick yesterday after you left."

He winced. "Sorry to hear that. Guess she'll be out of commission for a bit."

"Not to mention we'll both have to keep her

51

from lifting or overdoing things for a while."

Brent smiled wanly. "She can be stubborn."

"We've been friends for years and yes, she is one of the most stubborn people I know. I'll keep you posted." Jennifer paused. "However, we have another situation. This is serious. I have no idea what I need to do at this point and need some advice."

Brent sat back in his chair and gave Jennifer his full attention. She sat down.

"You know most of this story, but I'll start from the top again. Yesterday, when Jeff, Marcia and I arrived at the cemetery we placed Mr. Larson on the lowering device. A flash of lightening and a rather loud bang of thunder sent us running back to the coach, Jeff to the van. As we sat for a couple of minutes waiting for the storm to pass over, our phones alerted the tornado warning. The storm had gone from zero to sixty in seconds, so we made a beeline out of there, and as you know, we came here. After we shut down the funeral home, it was about five hours before I could get back to the cemetery. Brent, there was no casket. The tornado had swept through." She crossed her legs and started swinging the top leg, her anxiety mounting.

"I've tried and tried to reach the manager and

two trips to the cemetery have been unsuccessful. I think I should I call the police. What would you do?"

Brent exhaled and rubbed his hand over his face. He stared at the floor, then shook his head.

"I'd call the police." He looked at Jennifer's stricken face.

"Facing the consequences of losing Mr. Larson scares me, but I have no choice."

"Why don't you call from here? I'll help you through it."

Jennifer nodded, her face reflecting her misery. Pulling out her phone she looked up the non-emergency number, put it on speaker and hit the call button. It was answered quickly.

Her palms sweaty and her heart pounding, she asked to speak to a constable and placed her phone on Brent's desk.

"May I ask what this is about?"

"A possible theft," she responded.

"One moment please."

All too quickly again, before she had a chance to think of what to say, it was answered.

"Constable Ayers."

Brent smiled encouragingly at her as Desta poked her head around the corner of the door and handed him Marcia's card to sign. He nodded his thanks and set it aside, concentrating on Jennifer's call.

"Hello Constable Ayers, my name is Jennifer Spencer. I own Spencer Funeral Home. Just before the tornado struck, my staff and I were placing a casket on a grave at Whispering Pines Cemetery. We were forced to leave quickly when the tornado alert sounded. When I returned to the cemetery the casket was gone." She stopped talking for a few seconds. She'd been holding her breath and had no more air to push the words out. Brent put his hand on her arm and gave it a quick squeeze.

"You're doing just fine," he whispered.

"Let me see if I understand you correctly, Ms. Spencer. You're are calling about a missing casket? Are you with a store that sells caskets?"

Jennifer raised her eyebrows and she and Brent exchanged "are you kidding me" looks. She shook her head at the constables' response and changed her tone, hoping she would sound more convincing.

"No Constable, I'm a funeral director. I own Spencer Funeral Home and Williams Funeral Home. The tornado interrupted a graveside service. The casket, with the deceased, is gone." This time her tone was firmer.

The pause stretched into long seconds.

"May I put you on hold?"

"Certainly."

"I shouldn't be surprised," she said to Brent quietly. "If I was that officer I wouldn't know what to say or do either."

Brent chuckled. "Once you adopted your 'boss' voice he took you seriously. Maybe he didn't know what funeral homes were in town. My first clue would have been your last name."

"Maybe missing caskets aren't part of their job description. What if they don't help? Brent didn't have time to answer her musing, the Constable was back.

"Ms. Spencer?"

"Yes?"

"We will send an officer to the funeral home shortly. Would 11:00 a.m. be acceptable?"

"It would, thank you." She tapped off and exhaled, her relief evident. "I hope we can get to the bottom of this today," she said.

His mouth twitched. "Or at least get the casket to the bottom of the..." He stopped mid-sentence. "Bad joke, sorry."

She smiled wryly. "I won't rest until Mr. Larson *is* at the bottom of the grave. If the media gets wind of this—" She stopped mid-sentence too and rolled her eyes.

It was Brent's turn to smile. "No matter what or how we say it, it becomes a bad joke. Don't worry, I won't tell anyone we had this conversation if you don't."

Brent turned to Marcia's card and read it. Chuckling, he signed it and handed it to Jennifer.

"Deal," she responded as she rose from her chair. "I'd better get going, I have one more stop to make before I get back, and Elaine wants to go to the hospital and drop off the card and basket for Marcia. I wish I had time to stop by and see her quickly. Maybe this evening. Oh yeah, one more thing. The coach is parked at the back of the lot at Spencers."

"Don't worry about it. Jeff and I can pick it up later."

As she opened the office door she turned to Brent. "Thanks for the support."

"Anytime. Keep me posted."

She left quietly through the back door and drove to Design A, anxious to get the repairs and renovations started. The store was on Main Street and she found a parking spot out front. The windows of the store looked into a bright and modern space. Lighting, furniture and accessories were detailed in groupings. She liked the modern feel as she looked through the windows. A chime sounded as she opened the door. A woman rose from a desk in the back and approached her as she looked around at the groupings of furniture.

"Hi, is there something I can help you with?"

Jennifer had predicted a pretentious designer, but this woman was warm and friendly. Having never dealt with a designer before she had the impression they were flamboyant and pushy. *Stop with the stereotypes, if that were true then the stereotypical funeral director is downright creepy.*

"I'm interested in a quote for some repairs, renovations and furniture," said Jennifer.

"Would you like to take a seat?" asked the woman pleasantly.

"Unfortunately, I'm pressed for time. Would it be possible to set up an appointment?"

"Of course, what space were you looking to have renovated?"

Jennifer pulled her card and handed it to the woman. "We had some damage to our lounge and one of the suites, and I would consider a quote for the kitchen area of the upstairs apartment. I may also consider expanding one of the office spaces."

The woman glanced at the card quickly. "I can

appreciate you need to get your business operable quickly. Perhaps we could meet at the funeral home. Would it be convenient for you after your business hours?" she asked.

"I appreciate your flexibility."

The woman smiled again. "Not a problem, may I stop by this evening?"

"5:30 p.m.?"

"I can do that, Ms. Spencer. I'll discuss this with my partner and we will see you later. My name is Carol." She extended her hand then turned to her desk. "Here's my card."

"Thank you." Carol's handshake was firm and she looked Jennifer straight in the eyes. She felt comfortable with this attractive and personable designer.

"See you later," Jennifer said as she left the store. She felt a tiny spark of excitement as she mentally pictured the new kitchen in her apartment and the office space off the lounge. As she climbed into the car, she scanned the card and tucked it into her wallet. Looking up as she noticed a man standing talking to Carol, his arms waving wildly.

Wonder what that's all about.

5

With a few minutes to spare, Jennifer parked the car beside the garage at the funeral home and went to the front office.

"Hi Elaine. Anything new?"

"No, nothing. Are you going to be here for a while?"

"I have a police officer coming to take a statement about Mr. Larson's disappearance, and Carol, from Design A, will be here this evening. Here's Marcia card, it just needs your signature."

"The basket is ready. I'll pick that up, visit Marcia briefly if I am allowed to see her, then I should stop at Williams. Desta and I have some stuff from last month to work on."

"Take your time, I'll let you know if something comes up."

Elaine put her jacket on and picked up her purse. "Do you want me to bring back lunch?"

"Why don't you get some for you and Desta. I'll grab a sandwich later if I'm hungry."

"OK, bye. Don't skip lunch!" Elaine said sternly as she disappeared out the front door. A quick check of her watch made Jennifer decide to heed Elaine's advice. She walked to her apartment stairs and bounded up them two at a time.

"Hi Grimsby," she called as she opened the door. He jumped off the back of the couch and rubbed up against her legs. Plucking him off the floor, she rubbed under his chin and behind his ears. She carried him to the kitchen, got a couple of cookies from the package in her cupboard and took a couple of treats from Grimsby's treat jar. He purred contentedly as she put them under his nose and left to go back downstairs.

Making herself a cup of tea, she'd barely finished the cookies when the door opened. "Right on time," she muttered as she entered the front hall.

A young constable stood inside the door, looking around uncomfortably. As she approached him she smiled warmly, made eye contact and extended her hand. He was tall, over six feet and had dark hair and brown eyes. He looked about nineteen years old.

"Jennifer Spencer."

He shook her hand like she was made of dust, his discomfort at the environment obvious.

"Constable Ayers."

"Let's have a seat." She started walking to the lounge. "Would you like tea, coffee?"

The Constable had not moved. When she turned back around, he startled.

"No, thank you."

Jennifer felt a bit sorry for him, remembering how Warren, one of her protection officers had reacted when she mentioned the morgue. She stood quietly waiting for the officer to join her. He looked around, taking in his surroundings.

"Is this your first visit to a funeral home?"

He nodded and cleared his throat. "Um, yes." His discomfort had clearly got the best of him.

"I appreciate you stopping by. The situation with Mr. Larson's casket is serious and I am very concerned."

She sat in her favourite chair and waited for him to take a seat. He seemed to visibly relax once he sat down and glanced around. The lounge was probably the least uncomfortable spot in the funeral home for him. She'd considered using the front office, but it was a bit clinical and formal with the computer and desk and seating. The lounge was a better choice, even if it was short a few pieces of furniture.

As he sat down, her phone cheeped. She pulled

it from her pocket and glanced at the text. It was Ryan, letting her know that Marcia had not improved and that her surgery was scheduled for 1:00 p.m. She texted back a sad face and *"ty"*.

"Sorry," she said to the young constable. "I put it on vibrate."

The constable seemed to be all arms and legs in the chair in front of her as he reached for his notebook, missing the pocket and fumbling for his pen.

"Yes, well, I have a few questions for you."

Jennifer nodded, not trusting herself to speak. The poor guy was rather awkward.

"When did you discover the missing casket?"

"After the tornado, about five hours after we had to leave the cemetery."

Not once did he look at her as he fired off a list of questions that he, or someone else, had prepared. His tone became almost cynical after ten minutes of non-stop questioning and note-taking, he didn't deviate once from his list. He finally looked at her.

"All this time and you haven't been able to reach the cemetery manager? How many times did you call?"

Jennifer had patiently answered his questions, sticking to facts until he asked about her attempts to contact the cemetery manager with undisguised scepticism. She straightened, pulled her shoulders back and looked him straight in the eye. It felt personal, as if he was questioning her integrity.

"The evening before the burial was the first call, I have a record of my other attempts on my phone." She opened the notepad app and handed him her phone. "If I knew where he lived I would have stopped by. It's not like him not to respond. I'm concerned about him. Do you have his address?"

The constable flushed a little as he looked at her record of calls. He replied in the affirmative. "He lives beside the cemetery, behind the stand of pine trees."

"Then I'll follow you over if you don't mind. Let me get my jacket." She stood, went to her office and put her funeral jacket on. She hit the call button for the answering service on her phone, "Hi, I'll be out of the funeral home for a while. I have my cell and pager. Thanks." She tapped off the call to the answering service, and walked to the front door to lock up. Then, as she turned and headed back to the garage door, with Constable Ayers trotting behind her, she texted Elaine to let her know she'd be out.

By the time the constable caught up to her, he didn't say anything as she closed up the back and clicked the unlock button for the car. Jennifer had her seatbelt done up and the car started by the time the constable made it to his vehicle.

The constable took his time radioing in. Jennifer drummed her fingers on the steering wheel impatiently while she waited. She watched as he answered his phone.

He must be brand new. His questions were stiff and scripted, and he seems to need to check in with someone at the station. This could take all day.

Eventually, he started the car and without even a glance in her direction, pulled out of the parking lot.

Jennifer followed leisurely behind him, her mind turning to her evening meeting with the decorator. At the intersection that led to the cemetery, the Constable turned signaled a right turn. Whispering Pines cemetery was to the left. Jennifer flicked on her left turn signal, hoping he would notice, but as the light changed he turned right. She decided he'd figure it out eventually and turned left.

Pulling into the cemetery, she drove to the gravesite. Nothing had changed. Driving back around to the cemetery entrance she saw a squad car racing down the highway, slowing when it reached the cemetery. He waved at her to follow him. About half of a kilometre away, behind the tall stand of trees, stood a white frame bungalow with a large garage, resembling a barn, in the back.

The Constable pulled into the driveway and parked behind the house, Jennifer right beside him.

She stood nearby, looking around the property while he radioed in. One of the garage doors was partially open, a black pickup truck protruding slightly. A padlock dangled opened on the door latch. The yard was littered with debris and branches.

"That's odd," she said when the Constable exited his car. "That pickup is partially in the garage and nothing has been cleaned up since the storm."

Without a backwards glance to see his reaction, she walked quickly toward the truck. As she got closer she saw a person slumped over the steering wheel. The Constable was standing where she'd left him: at the door to his car, his nose in his notebook, scribbling furiously.

"Over here!" she yelled as she ran the remaining few feet to the garage. She yanked open the driver's side door and reaching up, touched the side of the man's neck, checking for a carotid pulse. "He's alive, but barely," she said. The Constable's long legs had helped him cover the distance quickly. His hand went his radio as he called for an ambulance. Jennifer stepped back and looked around the garage.

The casket containing Mr. Larson was in the back of the truck. Torn between relief and concern, she turned her attention back to the cemetery manager.

"His pulse is thready, and he is not breathing well," she told the Constable after he had radioed the directions for the ambulance. "He must have been here since the tornado." She felt herself tremble and reached up to touch the shoulder of the unconscious man.

"Mr. Cameron. Mr. Cameron, can you hear me? Help is on the way." He was a portly man who looked to be in his mid-fifties. He did not respond.

In the distance, she could hear an approaching siren. As the constable walked to the edge of the road to direct the ambulance, she noticed a pickup truck on the highway and watched as it slowed down to pull into the driveway. The Constable tried to flag it down, but the driver continued around the squad car, across the grass and through the yard to the garage. He slammed it into park and leapt out of his vehicle, running towards Jennifer.

"What happened? Is Doug alright?"

"He's alive, we just found him."

She stepped aside as the man moved to the driver's side door. "Doug, buddy, hang in there." He turned to Jennifer.

"Oh man, oh man," he said, running his hands through his hair over and over. "I should have checked on him." He was clearly distraught.

"Are you a friend?"

"Friend and neighbour. We've known each other since grade school. We always, always had each other's back. I help him at the cemetery sometimes. Oh man. This can't be happening."

The siren cut off as the ambulance pulled into the driveway. Jennifer took the man's arm and steered him gently off to the side. They watched quietly as the paramedics took Doug out of the vehicle and started an IV.

"How long has he been in the truck?" asked one of the paramedics, as he continued his examination. The other paramedic had started an IV and was placing leads on his chest and ankles.

"Since the tornado probably," replied the constable.

"Let's go," said the paramedic who'd placed the leads. Jennifer could see from the monitor that Doug's heartrate was erratic. Moving quickly, the paramedics loaded him into the ambulance and left for the hospital, siren screaming. Jennifer and the manager's friend watched the ambulance pull away. Turning to him, she introduced herself.

"I'm Jennifer."

"Ronnie." He shook his head. "I should have checked on him. I thought he was busy or went to bed early. Oh man." He started pacing again.

"Is this the missing casket?" The sharp tone of voice startled them.

Both Jennifer and Ronnie turned and stared at the Constable, the surprise at his lack of empathy reflecting on their faces.

"It is," said Jennifer quietly. She felt like adding, "but it can wait." The abrupt and insensitive young constable was starting to annoy her. After a short pause, she did say it but the constable didn't hear her, he'd gone to the back of the garage to look at the casket in the truck bed. Ronnie did hear her.

"Doug must have brought the casket here because of the storm. He would have used the lift on the tractor to raise it off the lowering device. He always parked his truck at the shed. Maybe with the storm being so violent he lowered the casket in the truck bed and brought it here. That shed wasn't as secure as his barn. It doesn't make sense though. Why didn't he just lower the casket into the grave and take cover?"

"Maybe he didn't want to leave the casket exposed to the rain? He wouldn't have had time to fill in the grave. The storm came so fast," Jennifer mused.

Ronnie nodded. "Maybe. He must have collapsed as he backed the truck in. I should have checked on him. I was too busy cleaning up my yard." He resumed his pacing, unaware that he was repeating himself.

"It's not your fault," said Jennifer firmly. He didn't seem to hear her. "Ronnie!" Her tone caused him to stop fretting and look at her.

"You had no way of knowing. He could have collapsed anywhere." The constable had rejoined them. He stood at the front of the pickup truck taking notes. He looked up at Ronnie.

"Are you the next of kin?"

"No. I'm his best friend. He doesn't have anyone, except a sister out west. His wife left him years ago."

The constable wrote down Ronnie's name and number, then turned to Jennifer.

"Well, Ms. Spencer. The casket has been located. I'm sure you can make arrangements to have someone take care of the burial."

"I can't leave the casket like this. Are you going to secure the garage?" she asked.

He wrinkled his nose. The truck seat was soiled

with urine. When Doug collapsed with his heart attack or stroke he'd lost control of his bodily functions, a normal part of such an event. It was obvious the constable did not want to back the truck up. Jennifer dealt with body fluids as part of her job. She felt little 'snap' in her brain. She was furious and had enough of his indifferent attitude.

"Never mind. I'll do it," she said, making no attempt to hide her disgust at his attitude. Looking around for a tarp or some kind of cloth, she saw one folded neatly on a work bench. She picked it up, partially unfolded it and put it on the seat. She grabbed the bar near the seatbelt and hoisted herself into the truck cab.

"Wait!" said Ronnie, stepping forward. "I've got my keys for the cemetery buildings. I can do the burial for you. I've got time."

From her perch in the truck cab, Jennifer was eye to eye with Ronnie. His weathered face showed his sincerity. She nodded slowly.

"Thank you, that's very kind of you."

"It's the least I can do to help you and Doug. I'll drive the truck over, you follow in your car."

He turned to the Constable, walked up to him and stood toe to toe. "Think you can lock the garage when we leave, young man?"

"What about the truck?"

"Don't you worry none about Doug's truck. I have keys. I'll lock the truck in the garage when I return. First thing I will do when I get back is go into Doug's house and feed his cat. Then I will lock that door. That OK with you officer?"

Jennifer felt a tiny bit of satisfaction at the disconcerted look on the constable's face. Ronnie was taking charge.

"Fine." Constable Ayers backed up a bit. Jennifer hopped out of the truck cab as Ronnie approached. He winked. She couldn't help but smile back at him.

"This won't take long," he said as he climbed into the cab. He started the truck and pulled out of the garage.

"Thank you, Constable Ayers," was all she said as she walked past him to her car, started the engine and pulled away, Ronnie ahead of her with Mr. Larson.

She pulled up behind the truck once they reached the grave and together they walked to the grave site. The two of them straightened out the lowering device and checked the ground for stability. The water that had been in the bottom of the grave the day before had seeped away.

"There's a church truck in the office. I'll go get it. It'll be easier if we wheel the casket over to the grave."

"I'll come too. Let me get the burial permit out of the car." Reaching into the glove compartment she pulled out the permit for Mr. Larson. Her fingers brushed the container of committal sand and she slipped it into her pocket. Marcia would be pleased to know the committal service was done. Her relief at the resolution of Mr. Larson's disappearance was enormous.

"That young officer has a few things to learn about life," said Ronnie as they walked to the office.

"Just like the rest of us did, and still do," said Jennifer lightly. Ronnie laughed.

"He'll learn soon enough I guess. When we are done here, can I buy you a coffee? Is Tim Horton's OK? I should go to the hospital to check on Doug."

"I'd love a coffee, but I insist on buying. My friend is having surgery today, I want to check on her as well. They have a Tim's in the hospital."

Jennifer left the burial permit in the top desk drawer and, between the two of them, they were able to get Mr. Larson to his final resting place.

"Do you mind if I take a few minutes to do a

burial service? It doesn't seem right to just walk away."

"Don't mind a bit." He stood beside her at the head of the grave and folded his hands respectfully. She pulled the committal sand from her pocket and handed it to him.

She recited the short committal service from memory and as she reached "ashes to ashes, dust to dust," Ronnie leaned in and made a cross. The two of them stood quietly for another minute before Ronnie handed back the committal sand and lowered the casket. She watched while he unlocked the shed and filled in the grave with the small tractor. After all the fiasco and the challenging situation with the Larsons, she felt a profound sadness for the dysfunctional family. Ronnie completed his task with the tractor and smoothed out the top of the grave with his shovel. He stood back and surveyed his work.

"There."

"Do you want to feed the cat before we meet up at the coffee shop?" asked Jennifer as they walked back to their vehicles.

"Yeah, I should do that. I'll drop the church truck in the office and lock up. Need to let my wife know what I'm up to. Lemme give her a call."

Jennifer checked her phone while Ronnie called his wife. He was at the window of her vehicle a few minutes later.

"Lori, my wife, is gonna feed the cat. Told her what I was doing, she said to thank you for finding Doug. I'll follow you to the hospital."

Jennifer waited at the roadway while he dropped off the church truck and locked the office. As they parked at the hospital, she asked Ronnie if he wanted to check with the Emergency Department before they had coffee.

"Yeah. He might still be there." Jennifer waited while Ronnie talked to the clerk in Emergency. She saw a nurse take him off to the side to update him. It was taking a few minutes and she looked around at the busy waiting room, full of all ages of injured and sick people. A tiny baby wailed as siblings played at a tired mother's feet. An old man dozed in a wheelchair. The room carried an odour of sickness.

"Jennifer!"

She turned to see Detective Sergeant Gillespie walking toward her.

"Ryan—how's Marcia?"

"I'm on my way up. She should be out of surgery by now. Are you going up to see her?"

"Eventually." She told him the story about the

casket and finding Doug, and Mr. Larson's burial in a few sentences.

Ryan chuckled. "I should start keeping a list of your graveside mishaps. This story is better than the last one." Jennifer's stomach sank. Ryan had reminded her of the dropped casket, an injured employee, a swooning widow and a pallbearer with a heart condition. The Werther interment had required two ambulances. She and Marcia had been humiliated and embarrassed at the situation *and* by the cemetery manager, Mr. Whitney. It was Ryan who had shown them the humour in it. There wasn't time to say anything more, Ronnie joined her. The relief on his face was evident.

"Ronnie, this is Detective Sergeant Gillespie. Ronnie buried Mr. Larson today. I am indebted to him."

As Ronnie shook hands with Ryan, his eyes crinkled with the hint of a smile.

"That young constable needs to step up a bit."

"How so?" asked Ryan amicably.

Ronnie gave him a quick rundown. Ryan looked at Jennifer. "Do you concur?" She hung her head, a little embarrassed by Ronnie's bluntness and nodded.

"Thanks. I'll look into it. What was his name?"

"Ayers," was Jennifer's short response. As Ryan

excused himself to check on Marcia as she looked intently at Ronnie.

"How's Doug?"

"He had a stroke. Oh man, how many times did I tell him to see a doctor? He wouldn't go and now he may never work again. My wife and I can handle the cemetery, but it was Doug's pride and joy. The nurse said they'll know more once he's conscious. He's in the ICU. I can have fifteen minutes with him."

"Do you want to have coffee first or after you visit?"

"Let's sit for a bit, it's been quite a shock."

She led the way to the coffee shop just off the Emergency Room waiting area. "I've got this," she told him as they found a table in the busy shop. Jennifer purchased the coffee and then sat across from Ronnie, who regaled her with stories of him and Doug growing up. The two buddies had not ventured far outside the Niagara region and Ronnie noted it might be a good idea to take a vacation further afield with his wife. Having his best friend in critical condition had given him a wake-up call. Finishing his coffee, he rose.

"I'm glad you found Doug when you did. Thanks for the coffee."

"You're welcome. You can't know how much I appreciate you taking the time to bury Mr. Larson. Thank you."

Jennifer stopped at the information desk to ask for Marcia's room, then took the elevator to the surgical floor. Marcia lay flat, covered with a sheet, sleeping. Her face looked pasty. Ryan was sitting quietly in the chair beside her.

Jennifer raised her eyebrows as she made eye contact with him.

"Surgery went well. She'll be going home later this evening if she isn't vomiting."

"Do you want me to drive her home?"

Ryan shook his head no. "I took a few days off, long overdue. I'll take care of her."

At the sound of their voices, Marcia opened her eyes and tried to focus on Ryan. Immediately he was on his feet, bending over her.

"How are you? Any pain?"

Marcia smiled through heavy eyelids. "I feel awesome. Amazing. Will you marry me?" She closed her eyes and drifted off again.

Ryan's crooked grin lit up his face. "Of course." He turned to Jennifer. "It's the drugs. That's the third time she's proposed. He chuckled happily.

"I hope you accepted her proposals," said

Jennifer jokingly. "Can I get you anything?"

"It's all good, but thanks." He looked at her closely. "And yes, I did accept her proposal."

"For sure?" Jennifer's eyes widened.

"For sure," was the firm reply. Without thinking, Jennifer threw her arms around him. He responded in kind.

"That's the best news I have had in weeks. You and Marcia are meant to be together. I'm so happy for you."

"Thanks." Ryan blushed.

"I can't wait to watch this unfold, but for now, I have to run. I appreciate you sharing your good news with me."

"You're the first to know, that's only right."

"Call me if you need anything, OK?"

"All right."

Jennifer drove back to the funeral home happier than she had felt in a long time. Marcia and Ryan were a great match. They understood the demands of their jobs, they didn't try to change each other, and their love was based on mutual respect. It had been a good day. Mr. Larson had been found and her best friend had chosen her life partner. She breathed a quick prayer for Doug.

Pulling into the parking lot at Spencer's with a few minutes to spare before the meeting with the design firm, Jennifer turned on most of the lights in the funeral home. She scooted upstairs to check on Grimsby's food and water and quickly surveyed the apartment to ensure it was tidy.

Right on time, Carol entered the funeral home, followed by the man Jennifer had seen arguing with her earlier in the day.

"Hello Carol, nice to see you again. I'm looking forward to seeing what you have to propose."

Once again, she was struck by Carol's warm smile. "I'd like you to meet my partner, Graham."

"Senior partner darling," said the man. Immediately the atmosphere cooled as Carol stiffened.

Jennifer quickly jumped in. "Nice to meet you, Graham." Her first impression was that he was pushy and arrogant as he looked around the lobby, his nose in the air.

"Shall we get started?"

Leading the way to the lounge Jennifer turned to Graham. "I outlined my ideas with Carol earlier today. This room is going to have the most drastic change. I'd like to refurbish and expand this little office into the selection room, this way." Opening the door to the selection room Jennifer led the two designers in. Again, Graham's nose went up slightly. He sniffed.

He's like a caricature of a designer. They do exist. I'll ignore him and work with Carol.

"Carol, my plan here is to expand the office into this space, adding at least two, maybe three workstations and a dividing wall with my office. I would like to expand my office to include comfortable seating so I can meet with staff and visitors. What do you think?"

"What will you do with all the caskets?"

"I'll be taking out a third or more of them. My other funeral home has basement storage and I can use video to display units, pulling from that site if I need them. Cremation is on the increase, urns don't take much room. Workspace for at least two directors is needed and my office could be used for preplanning space." Graham straightened up at the words "my other funeral home". Jennifer could almost see dollars signs in his eyes.

"That sounds like a good plan. We could separate your office with glass, put curtains or blinds up so you could close them if you want privacy," Carol suggested, taking notes.

"I never thought of that, what a great idea,"

Jennifer said.

"Not so fast darling," said an irritated Graham, looking at Carol. She held his gaze for a few seconds before dropping her head.

Jennifer was not impressed with his attitude. "What do you propose Graham?" Carol's tone, although respectful, had a touch of ice.

"We move the lounge into this room and use the existing lounge for offices and caskets. That would more than double the lounge space."

"How would clients access the lounge?" asked Carol politely.

"Why through the urns and caskets of course," he responded with distain. "Isn't that what people buy in a funeral home?"

Jennifer bit her lip, willing herself not to snap at him. She wanted to ask him if he had a previously bad experience with funeral homes. Clearly, he had no sense of how visitations and chapel services worked. The lounge was a gathering place for a quick coffee and chat, the suites were where clients visited with family and friends and spent most of their time.

Oh heck. He is not the client, I am. Stand up to him.

"Graham, have you had a bad experience with a

funeral home in the past? Have you designed any funeral homes?"

There, I said it.

He was clearly taken aback by her bluntness. Jennifer detected a hint of a smile on Carol's face.

"Well, no, but it's all about sales isn't it?"

"No, it is not." She could feel her ire rising and with effort, she softened her tone. "It's about giving people a place to feel safe in their grief. The flow through the funeral home has to work for the staff as well. The selection room is off limits to visitors which means the lounge stays here."

She turned to Carol. "I think it's important to soundproof the walls between the office and lounge and selection room."

"Agreed." Carol turned her back on Graham, who clearly did not like being ignored. He folded his arms across his chest and tapped his foot.

"That is the main renovation. There are a few drywall repairs to be done in the lounge. I'm thinking of replacing the existing club chairs with something similar. Let's look at the large suite, it also needs drywall repair, paint, a carpet, and some new furniture."

Carol continued to take notes as she listened carefully to what Jennifer was saying. When they finished in the suite, they headed upstairs to the apartment, Graham in tow. Grimsby stretched and yawned, rubbing up against Jennifer's legs. When Graham reached down to pet him, Grimsby jumped aside, his back arched. Graham backed off. Several times he interrupted with his ideas, all outrageous, all costly. Jennifer continued to ignore him, turning back to Carol every time he distracted her with his plans.

"Here is a photo of what I picture the kitchen to be. I'd like an island with chairs, and new cupboards and countertop. The appliances are not energy efficient, the stove is twenty years old. I'm open about paint colour. And the existing deck area is a good size, but can it be screened in?"

After a good back and forth discussion with Carol and a few interruptions from a jittery Graham, Jennifer led the two designers back downstairs. Standing at the door Carol checked her notes.

"I can have some sketches, samples and an estimate of tradespeople tomorrow or the next day. May I come back with our assistant at your convenience to take measurements tomorrow? I should have some quotes for you by then as well and if you approve, get the contract signed."

"Of course, I'll be here in the morning."

"In that case, Agnes and I will stop by around ten."

"Thank you, Carol, you have some great ideas. Nice meeting you Graham."

She'd barely locked the door behind them when she heard an argument break out. Peaking discretely out the window she watched Graham erupt, his arms waving as he walked with Carol to their vehicle. *Graham may be the senior partner, but he has an over-inflated sense of importance. Carol and I will work well together. Hopefully, he won't be around too much.*

6

The next few days passed quickly as Carol submitted the estimate and hired the tradespeople. Elaine and Jennifer watched the design work unfold with interest as walls were torn down and new ones were framed in.

Agnes, Carol's assistant, was in and out measuring and delivering information to Jennifer. A quiet, mousy-looking woman, Agnes seemed older than she looked. Her long skirts, peasant blouses and light brown hair reaching her waist seemed to drag her down. Jennifer had observed her take measurements and notes and had to admit she was efficient. Agnes kept her measuring tape hanging around her neck as she worked, tying it in an interesting knot to keep it in place.

Carol and Agnes appeared to work well together and Carol was respectful with everyone. As the various tradespeople came in, it was clear that they liked her as well. The only time the situation changed was when Graham showed up. He went out of his way to criticize Carol's work, her choice of colour and materials and her design. At those moments, Agnes seemed to fade into the woodwork and the tradespeople ignored him.

"There's something about Graham that doesn't sit well with me," Elaine said quietly to Jennifer after a particularly loud exchange. "I wonder if he is on drugs, he's so jittery and volatile."

"I wondered the same thing. Carol seems to be the driving force behind the company."

Carol's main focus was getting the lounge done first, then the suite and offices. The apartment was to be left until the main floor was completed. Jennifer and Elaine enjoyed sitting with her, pouring over catalogues, picking colours and looking at swatches.

Marcia called two days after her surgery. Jennifer was surprised at how chipper her friend was.

"I feel great," she said in response to Jennifer inquiry. "When all that pain and vomiting started I wanted to die. Seriously. It was horrible. I woke up after the surgery and it was as if nothing had happened. I'm a bit uncomfortable if I try and do too much, but honestly, I had no idea I'd feel this good so soon. The surgeon said I could go back to work in a week if I do light duty. I have a couple of tiny incisions that are healing nicely, that's all. My mom was laid up for weeks when she had her gallbladder out."

"Is Ryan still looking after you?"

She chuckled. "Ryan would make a great nurse, he is so attentive."

"Congratulations by the way," said Jennifer. "I hear Ryan accepted your proposal."

"He says I proposed three times. I only remember one."

"Do you remember him saying yes?"

"Vaguely, mostly I remember him taking care of me. Even the nurses were impressed. I can't wait to show you the ring he got me, it's not what you'd expect. He said he got it a month ago, he was going to ask me to marry him."

"I can't wait to see it! Have you set a date?"

"Not yet. We're in no hurry. Between you and me, I think we might slip off to a Justice of the Peace. We can always have a party for our friends and family down the road. I haven't had this condo very long, Ryan is happy in his place. If we can get approval from the condo board we might make it one large unit. It's been fun making wedding plans, then changing them. Neither of us wants to fuss with a big event."

"I am so happy for both of you. I haven't told

anyone else about your engagement, that's your job."

"You do know you're my maid of honour, right?"

"I'd be thrilled and honoured. Who did Ryan pick for best man?"

"Guess," said Marcia.

"I have no idea, one of the team?"

"Sort of," coached Marcia.

"Umm, the Lieutenant?"

"Not even close!"

"There's one person I think he might pick. They've been through a lot together, but I could be wrong, he moved on."

"Well?"

"Jim?"

"You guessed it!"

"That makes sense. They worked together for a long time." Jennifer remembered Jim telling her about his struggle with PTSD, when he was one of her protection officers. Jim had moved on to work with the security team for the Wisener companies. Mr. Wisener had been Jennifer's client when his son died. She was pleased to hear that Ryan had chosen Jim, and was looking forward to seeing him again.

"I think I might pop in for a visit on Monday if

you aren't busy, and stay for a couple of hours, see how I feel."

"That's a great idea. You'll be able to see the new office area.

"So you hired a firm? How are the designers working out?"

"Great, with one exception."

"I'm all ears."

"I hired Design A. The senior designer, Graham, is not someone I find endearing. His ideas are way out there and he's a volatile prima donna. His partner, Carol, on the other hand, is a kindred spirit. You'll like her. She listens, she adapts and she's good at her job. We should have the suite finished by the end of the week and the offices within a week. Part of the wall between my office and the selection room has been taken down and the new one is roughed in. The apartment will be last, there's no hurry. Carol's a powerhouse, we are actually ahead of schedule."

Jennifer looked up to see Elaine standing at the door making motions.

"Elaine just poked her head into my office, we have a call. I'll catch you later."

"Bye!"

It was the social services clerk from city hall,

notifying her they had an indigent burial. Jennifer took the details, thanked the clerk, and called the hospital. The body had been released. She called the city cemetery, the one Mr. Whitney managed, to order the grave. They informed her it would be ready tomorrow morning. She reached Chaplain Clive at the hospital and he agreed to do a graveside service.

"I'm going to the hospital, can you help me put a casket in the prep room?" she asked Elaine, who'd been watching the workmen.

The two of them uncovered the casket, the least expensive one in the selection room in accordance with social services criteria. The room was disorderly, all the caskets that had not been moved to Williams Funeral Home for storage were covered with plastic or cloth as the workers rebuilt part of the wall between the lounge and the selection room. Agnes, who was talking with one of the workmen, glanced over with interest as Elaine and Jennifer moved the casket. Jennifer made sure the back door to the selection room was locked before she and Elaine opened the prep room door and put the casket inside.

"I should be back in about a half hour, the details are on my desk." The phone rang again, and Elaine left to answer it.

After Jennifer checked the supplies in the van and opened the garage door, she walked outside and took in the fresh cool air of early winter. Driving to the hospital she unrolled her window and hummed to herself. Happy that Marcia was recovering well and pleased with the start of the renovations, she took in her surroundings. *The memory of the kidnapping must have affected my mood more than I realized. I'm starting to feel like my old self again.*

After parking the van, she walked through the hospital to the Admitting office to pick up the death certificate. While she waited for the clerk to finalize the paper work she stared out the window and saw Ronnie walking toward the front door of the hospital. Thanking the admitting clerk, she quickly scribbled her signature, tucked the medical certificate into her pocket, and walked fast to catch up to him.

"Hi Ronnie, how are you? How's Doug?" A woman walked up to him and handed him a parking slip.

"Hi Jennifer, this is my wife, Lori."

Lori smiled warmly and extended her hand. "Nice to meet you."

"You too."

"Doug is the same, he hasn't responded yet," said Ronnie sadly. "The doctor told me today that if he does recover he could be in a long-term care facility for the rest of his life. The township has given Lori and me the job of managing the cemetery. Lori's going to do the books."

"We have Doug's cat, she's settling in." Lori looked up at her husband. "We can tell she misses him, she sits in the window for hours looking across at his house and watching for him."

"I'm sorry, that's so sad," Jennifer said. "He's such a nice man."

Ronnie nodded, tears forming. Lori squeezed her husband's arm, then turned to Jennifer.

"Do you have a business card Jennifer? There's nothing on file in the office. Doug preferred working outside, the office isn't the most organized, I couldn't find anything with your address and phone number."

"Right here." She pulled out a business card and handed it to Lori. Her phone cheeped, she excused herself and checked it. "I'd better get moving, take care you two."

It was Brent texting her to ask if he could come by and discuss his choice of funeral director for Williams. Unable to find the time to join him via teleconference, she'd told him to go ahead with the interviews. She texted in the affirmative and told him she'd meet with him in half an hour.

As she walked to the morgue she pulled out the death certificate and checked the name and cause of death. The name on the death certificate was John Doe. John and Jane Doe deaths always troubled her, she hated that people could be only a number, forgotten and unloved or lost and alone.

Brent pulled into the funeral home parking lot as she was backing the van into the garage and he helped her transfer the deceased to the prep room. She unlocked the back door to the selection room to see Carol, looking professional and pretty in a white blouse and blue pencil skirt, talking to the electrician. She had her fuchsia measuring tape draped around her neck, the splash of colour adding a bit of cheer.

Carol looked up as Brent and Jennifer passed through the room and smiled at the two of them. Jennifer introduced Brent quickly. She didn't stop to chat, the messy lounge and selection room were a deterrent to the work they had ahead of them and she knew the tradespeople were on a deadline.

After pouring coffee, Jennifer and Brent went into a suite away from the construction noise, to discuss the resumes. Finding a comfortable spot to sit, Brent broached the topic first.

"Two to choose from, a man and a woman." He passed both resumes to Jennifer, who scanned them quickly.

"You spoke with both of them?"

"I did. And I liked both of them. I don't want to influence your choice though. What do you think?"

She sat back in the chair and took a sip of her coffee. "To be honest with you, I think the gentleman will be the best candidate. My reasoning is simple, if we add another woman at this point it'll leave us with three female directors and one male. You have an apprentice coming in about five months, male or female, of course, that hasn't been decided as yet. Peter will be coming here, although I think both apprentices should spend equal time in each funeral home. In the end, though, it's your decision."

"I agree, a balanced senior staff makes sense. When I spoke with our female candidate, she did say she had several other interviews pending. I'm sure she'll have no trouble finding a job."

After talking to Brent about the mundane details like purchases and maintenance, she asked him if he thought Design A might be able to spruce up some areas of Williams' Funeral home.

"Hmm, I'll think about that. Desta might have a better idea of what could be done, her artistic skills far surpass mine. Right now, I want to get our new director hired and settled in."

As Jennifer stood, Brent picked up both cups and they walked together to the lounge.

"Any chance you could send Jeff over at 9:00 a.m. tomorrow to help with the graveside service?" she asked.

"Jeff's off tomorrow, will I do?"

"Come to think of it, we're the only two left, so I guess you'll just have to do," she said with mock sincerity. The two of them laughed together. Being short-staffed was nothing new. Having a new funeral director and the two apprentices down the road would be a luxury.

"Why don't I come in early, I can help you dress and casket Mr. Doe."

"Thanks, I appreciate the help. Chaplain Clive will be here a few minutes before nine. That means we can be at the cemetery by 9:30."

"My pleasure."

"I added a bonus to your cheque this week," said Jennifer, changing the subject. "You've picked up a lot of the slack with Marcia being sick, and during the situation with Travis. Ideally, since you are a manager, I'd like to see you work a 'normal' day so you can spend more time with your family.

That has not been happening. When Marcia returns and the new director starts, I'd like you to cut back your hours."

"Now I know why I took this job," Brent joked. "Truthfully though, funeral service is not a nine-to-five profession. Julie's used to my long hours, she knew it would be this way when she married me. I appreciate that you want me to cut back. Let's get through Christmas, since that is our busiest season, then I'll think about reducing my hours."

"Are you happy with the way Williams is going? Is there anything you'd like to change?"

"There are several possibilities, one might be an event centre. With the garages at the back no longer in use, there's room to expand. If one of the properties adjacent to the funeral home was to go up for sale, and if the city approved, I think there's potential there. Post funeral receptions, large visitations, maybe even community organizations can use that space.

Jennifer nodded thoughtfully.

"Since you moved some of your stock over to Williams, I took a closer look at what you're doing with the interactive display. If clients want to see the casket we can send it over, but I suspect that in time, it'll be the way many families chose a casket, short of buying it elsewhere and providing it themselves. I'd be interested in pursuing the interactive option at Williams as well."

"Agreed."

"Right now, though, I need to get staff up to speed and build a team. By this time next year, I think I should have accomplished it."

Jennifer nodded. "I've been thinking about a pre-planning director, someone close to retirement who could be available on a part-time basis to work between the two funeral homes."

"We're able to maintain the status quo, so to speak, with our current staff. Perhaps, in time, a pre-arrangement director might work.

"You're right," mused Jennifer. "We need to move ahead slowly, not rush."

A commotion distracted Jennifer and Brent. "Miss Carol, she told me to do this."

Graham's angry voice interrupted the workman. "And I am telling you this just won't do. Where is she?"

"She's at the back, Mr. Graham," they heard the workman say.

Jennifer looked at Brent and shook her head. Graham's yelling could be heard all through the funeral home as he started in at Carol.

Brent followed Jennifer to the selection room where, true to form, Graham was in the middle of a temper tantrum, waving his arms as he accentuated his point.

"Graham!" Jennifer said loudly.

He stopped shouting and looked at her.

"This is a funeral home. If you can't control your temper and keep your voice down I will have to ask you to leave. In fact, I would prefer you leave now."

With Brent standing beside her, Graham stared at both of them, swaying slightly. Without a word he brushed past her, muttering to himself as he exited the building.

Carol was close to tears. The awkward silence in the room eased slowly as the workmen turned back to their tasks.

"I am so sorry," she said. "He doesn't listen."

"It's not your fault. Don't worry about it. It'd be nice if he left you alone to do your job."

"It would be nice if he left me alone, period," muttered Carol in a voice so low Jennifer barely heard her. Jennifer walked Brent to the lobby, then let Elaine know she was going upstairs. She wanted to get away from the noise of the construction and clutter and take a break.

She spent the rest of the afternoon with Grimsby beside her, finishing off her business course and starting a new one. She watched the workmen leave as it got dark. As she cleaned up the kitchen after a quiet dinner, she observed Carol getting into her car, the last one to leave. She went downstairs, turned out a few lights, and ensured the doors were locked. On her way upstairs to her apartment, she called her twin, Anne.

"Yes?"

Jennifer couldn't keep the smile out of her voice. Her twin knew it was her and always answered like she was in the newsroom.

"How are things?" Jennifer asked.

"Busy. You?"

"Busy too. Have you talked to mom lately?"

"No, why?"

"Just wondering. I did speak to her a few weeks ago, she basically cut me off."

"Exactly, which is why I don't call her."

"You don't call me much either and I don't cut you off." Jennifer laughed. "Any chance you can get away for a romp around Niagara Falls for a few days?"

Anne's tone softened, "That sounds like a plan. I might be able to. I could check on the cottage, maybe stay there. One of our newsroom staff said they enjoyed visiting the place in the Falls where they have all the birds. Sounds like fun."

The two of them talked and laughed for over an hour, ending the conversation with an agreement that Anne would call when she could get away.

With an early start the next morning, Brent and Jennifer had completed dressing and casketing John Doe by the time Chaplain Clive arrived. Although there was technically no need to use the funeral coach, Brent brought it anyway. John Doe would not have to be taken to his final resting place in the van.

Jennifer drove with Chaplain Clive in her car, Brent followed with the hearse. At the cemetery, Jennifer walked ahead to check the grave while Chaplain Clive waited with Brent as he unloaded the church truck. It was a cloudy cold day with a strong hint of snow in the air, a far cry from the tornado weather of a few days ago. Jennifer wrapped her coat tighter around her as she walked to the grave, her head down against the wind.

As she approached, she noticed the boards which would normally have been across the grave were off to the side. They should have been in place, with the straps rolled up nearby ready to use to lower the casket. The straps looked as if they'd been kicked aside. It wasn't like the cemetery staff to be so careless.

As she reached the grave, it became immediately clear what happened. A man lay at the bottom of the grave. She sucked in her breath.

"Brent!" The wind snatched her words away. She turned back towards the funeral coach. "Brent!"

She saw him look up and start walking toward her. Her legs began to tremble.

Brent was at her side quickly, Chaplain Clive right behind her.

"Uh oh," was all he said. Jennifer backed up as Brent jumped down into the grave and checked the man's pulse. He looked up at the concerned faces of Chaplain Clive and Jennifer, and shook his head. Chaplain Clive reached over to help him out of the grave.

"He's dead." Brent brushed the dirt off his suit and coat as a shaking Jennifer reached into her pocket and pulled out her phone. She could see the cemetery truck pulling up with two cemetery workers who were there to assist with the burial. Heart pounding, she dialed 911 and gave the dispatcher the details and the location as Brent walked to the truck to notify the cemetery workers.

Taking one last look down, she saw a flash of fuchsia and took a closer look.

It was Graham, the designer, a measuring tape knotted tightly around his neck.

7

Mr. Whitney, the cemetery manager, arrived slightly ahead of the police. He spoke with his crew before approaching Brent and Jennifer. Ever pompous and particular, he strode purposefully across the grass, looking like a character from a 1950's movie set, minus the hat.

"Ms. Spencer, Mr. Vaughn, this event is most unfortunate." His whiny voice sent a shudder down Jennifer's spine.

Jennifer had already suggested to Brent that they not let Mr. Whitney know they knew the deceased.

"It is," Jennifer responded sincerely and politely. After Mr. Whitney had criticized her and Marcia over their career choice when they had the incident with the Werther funeral, the two of them distanced themselves by avoiding or minimizing any conversation with the manager. Marcia had sarcastically made the comment the day Jennifer purchased Williams Funeral Home that Mr. Whitney would be apoplectic when he found out she was the owner of two funeral homes. She had her doubts whether it would change his attitude.

"Once the police have completed their interview with me I would like to ensure Mr. Doe is removed from here," said Brent.

"Would you like to place Mr. Doe in the cemetery vault until the police give the go-ahead for burial?" asked Mr. Whitney. "It might be a day or so before the police allow us to proceed. This is highly unprecedented." He looked at Jennifer as he made his last statement. She felt a tiny twinge of guilt, as if it were her fault.

"It's up to the boss," said Brent as he turned to Jennifer, the beginning of a tiny smile playing at the corners of his mouth, his eyes twinkling as he looked down at her. Jennifer straightened her shoulders and addressed the cemetery manager.

"That is very kind of you. We can return to complete the graveside service as soon as we have permission from the police. Thank you, Mr. Whitney."

As Jennifer related to Marcia later, that picture would have been worth more than a thousand words. Mr. Whitney looked at Brent, then back to Jennifer. It was at that moment it dawned on him, Jennifer was the owner of the two funeral homes in town, and Brent worked for her. The little mean streak in her that she always tried hard to hide was delighted. Mr. Whitney wouldn't dare criticize or minimize her again. Brent had set him up beautifully. She allowed herself to gloat briefly before she brought herself back to the sobering reality in front of her.

"I'm sure the officer in charge will allow us to remove Mr. Doe to the vault right away," Brent said as he handed Mr. Whitney the burial permit.

"Thank you." Mr. Whitney took the permit. "I'll be at the office." A slightly diminished cemetery manager returned to his vehicle, and Brent and Jennifer watched the staff follow him back down the road.

As the responding officers placed the crime scene tape, Jennifer puzzled over the situation. Other than the boards and straps out of place, it wasn't clear how someone or someones had put him in the grave. The grass, didn't show footprints and there were no drag marks from the road. The gates were locked at night so how did the murderer get into the cemetery and not disturb anything?

Much to Jennifer's surprise, Detective Sergeant Gillespie pulled into the gates and parked just off the road. The second he stepped out of the cruiser, he was all business.

"Lock this cemetery gate and place an officer outside it to reroute cars around to the front of the cemetery." The constable he spoke to nodded and complied. Ryan checked the grave, then glanced around, finally approaching the three of them.

"You found the body?" *He's all business. Work mode.* She could relate.

"We did," she said. "How is Marcia?"

Ryan looked a little startled at her question.

"Doing well. She's up and about. I was only going to work for a few hours today, looks like I might be longer."

"I can stop by and check on her once we're free to leave. Which leads me to another question. The casket is still in the coach, I may have to place it in the cemetery vault until the scene is clear. Any idea how long that might be?"

"Maybe tomorrow, depends on what we find," said the Detective Sergeant.

"Mr. Whitney said those exact words. The vault will be locked."

A tiny smile flashed across Ryan's face, making him look boyish and mischievous. He had ribbed Marcia and Jennifer mercilessly about the Werther incident and Mr. Whitney's comment at the time.

"I will need your statements. I can start with whoever is driving the hearse, then you can remove the deceased."

"That would be me," said Brent. He followed the Detective Sergeant a discrete distance from Jennifer and the chaplain.

Jennifer turned to Chaplain Clive. "Let's wait in the car, hopefully, we'll get you back to the hospital soon."

"Not a problem," the always pleasant Chaplain Clive responded. She opened the door of her car for the chaplain. Once inside, she turned the heat on low.

"Damp it is," said Chaplain Clive. Jennifer loved his Scottish accent and nuances. "Finding that poor man in the grave was a wee bit disconcerting wouldn't you say?"

"To put it mildly. It startled me. I was too scared to scream." She laughed weakly. They chatted comfortably for the twenty minutes it took for Ryan to finish questioning Brent.

"Ryan has a few questions for the chaplain," said Brent as Jennifer lowered her window. "I'll take Mr. Doe to the vault and come back."

"You can have the lead car, Brent. I'll take the coach back to Williams. Since I was first on the scene, I suspect I'll be asked the same questions over and over with different twists." She turned and smiled at the chaplain. "Thank you, Chaplain Clive."

"You are most welcome, my dear. Call me when you are ready for the committal. I like to finish what I've started." He smiled broadly back at Brent and Jennifer, then went off to meet with the Detective Sergeant.

"Be right back," Brent said. Jennifer watched as he manoeuvred the coach around the police vehicles and drove toward the cemetery office. Still puzzled and curious about the fact that the grass leading to the grave did not appear to be disturbed, she opened the car door and stepped up, balancing on the edge of the seat, making herself as tall as she could. She scanned the area from the road to the grave. Nothing. She stepped back down, closed the car door and walked away from the front of the car a bit, checking for signs of drag marks. Again, nothing. The grass was pristine.

Maybe the person carried Graham to the grave. She shuddered as she realized the last time she saw Graham was less than twenty-four hours ago.

Brent had barely returned when Detective Sergeant Gillespie finished with the chaplain. Jennifer watched Brent and Chaplain Clive drive away, then waited beside the coach until Ryan was ready to interview her. He took his time checking the scene again, talking with the forensics officers, examining every detail. Pulling out his notebook, he made a few notes, then looked up at Jennifer and walked over to her.

"I would like to conduct this interview at the station. Can you meet me there in a couple of hours?"

"Certainly, Detective Sergeant," she responded, respectful of his position and authority. Off duty he was Ryan.

"You are next in line for the coroner's calls," continued the DS, "However, after my discussion with Brent, I believe it would be prudent if both you and Brent abstain from this transfer. In the meantime, I'd ask you to not discuss this case with him, or anyone else."

"Of course." *Uh oh. My confrontation with Graham right before he died has put me on the suspect list. Ryan knows I didn't, couldn't, kill him but he has to follow protocol.*

He checked his watch. "1:00 p.m." He walked away before she could respond.

"1:00 p.m. it is," she muttered to herself as she climbed into the funeral coach and started it. She chose to use the front exit of the cemetery rather than have the police let her out. Once at the gate, she hit the Bluetooth button and called Marcia.

"Hi Jen!"

"Hey, how are you?"

"A little bored. I want to go back to work. Ryan started back today. I miss him already."

Jennifer smiled at the forlorn note in Marcia's voice.

"I might be able to pop over later if that's OK with you?"

"Are you kidding me?" she squealed. "Of course! I can make dinner."

"You can? You sure?" Jennifer teased.

"Of course, silly. I'm fine."

"Sounds good, I have a busy afternoon so it might be close to six before I get there, that is, if I don't get a call."

"I'll keep my fingers crossed. If you do get a call, I'll keep dinner warm. See you later."

As soon as Jennifer parked the coach at Williams, she went inside to retrieve her keys. She said a quick hello to Desta and found Brent in his office.

"Close the door," he said when she poked her head around the corner.

"I can't talk to you about the case," she said as

she complied.

"I kind of figured that," he responded. "I suspect you won't be able to do the coroner's call for Graham's transfer either?"

She shook her head no.

"Jeff and I can take care of it."

She shook her head again.

"Really? I wonder why."

Jennifer looked at him and made a can't-discuss-it face and shrugged.

"I wasn't given instructions not to discuss it, but I'll let it go. I will tell you that I was truthful."

"You could be nothing less and I respect you for it. By the way, I like how you dealt with Mr. Whitney, deferring to me and calling me boss."

He laughed heartily. "Wasn't it fun to see his face when the lightbulb went on and he realized you owned both funeral homes? I'm glad I was there to witness it. He's so pompous. I suspect this means he'll treat you and Marcia with more respect."

"I hope so, and I have you to thank for it. Ryan and Marcia will enjoy the story, can't wait to tell them."

"Don't be surprised if I keep doing it. He's constantly setting himself up."

"It's wicked of me, but I look forward to it."

"I went ahead and contacted Gordon Wilson, the funeral director we talked about. He's willing to start next week."

"That *is* good news. Marcia will be in and out for about ten days before she comes back full-time. We can have a dinner to welcome him at one of the restaurants that has a view of the falls. I'll check with you closer to his start date, it would be nice if your wife could join us. He's single, correct?"

"Yes, he told me his girlfriend wasn't too happy about his move, but he wanted to get out of Ottawa and he has relatives in Niagara. She's a nurse and is looking for work here."

"As soon as I hear that we can proceed with the interment, I'll let you and Chaplain Clive know. It was nice of him to follow through with John Doe's burial." Jennifer excused herself and went back to Spencer's. Would Carol be there? Did she and Agnes know Graham was dead?

The first thing Jennifer did when she got back to the funeral home was find Elaine and tell her about the delay with the social service burial. While she was not supposed to discuss finding Graham dead, Elaine, as a staff member, needed the details in the event another call came in. She closed the door to the front office and sat down.

"We got a nasty shock at the cemetery today. When I went to check the grave, there was a body in it.

Elaine grimaced.

"It was Graham. He was murdered."

Elaine took a minute to process what Jennifer had said. "No surprise there. I suspect he had a few enemies. How awful for you though."

Jennifer smiled weakly. "It was a shock. I'm not to discuss it with anyone, of course, but you are part of the 'need to know' group."

"So we can't discuss suspects?"

"Theoretically, no. Why? Did you have someone in mind?"

Elaine pondered her statement before responding. "A drug dealer who wanted to get paid? Someone he owed money too?"

Jennifer shrugged. "Maybe. It would make sense. I have to go to the police station and give a statement shortly."

Walking into the lounge after her discussion with Elaine, Jennifer was surprised to see it was business as usual. The drywall between the office and lounge and selection room was in place. Jennifer walked into the new office, pleased to see it was a comfortable size, at least three times larger than her old office.

"Hi Jennifer!"

She turned around to see Carol. *Stay calm, look benign. Carol could be a suspect and you don't want her to know you found Graham.*

"Hi Carol, I see that you've made some good progress since yesterday."

"It's coming along nicely. We should be ready to paint in here in a few days. The suite is done. The furniture for that space should be here shortly. Agnes is cleaning it up. She's a neat freak. It'll be spotless."

Either she doesn't know about Graham or she's a good actress.

"Come see." Leading Jennifer into the suite, Carol stepped back at the door to let Jennifer go in first. Agnes looked up from her vacuuming as they entered and waved at them. The walls were brighter and the solid colour in new carpet changed the look of the room, making it appear less *busy*.

"Looks good. Can't wait to see the new furniture in place. It will have to wait though, I have a meeting in less than an hour."

"Then we'll see you when you get back," Carol said.

As Jennifer went upstairs to get a sandwich and a cup of tea, she wasn't so sure. She noticed Carol didn't have her fuchsia measuring tape measure draped around her neck, nor had she seen it anywhere as they walked through the renovations.

Grimsby greeted her, purring and wrapping himself around her legs. She scooped him up and cuddled him. *It can't be Carol, she's kind and friendly. Why would she kill her partner?* Jennifer muddled it over while she had lunch. Her meeting with Detective Sergeant Gillespie didn't worry her, she had nothing to hide. She hoped the truth would not result in Carol's arrest. Things did not look good for the friendly, hard-working designer.

Jennifer arrived at the station promptly at 1:00 p.m. The Constable at the desk informed her that Detective Sergeant Gillespie was running a little late. She sat in the waiting room, tapped her reading app and immersed herself in a book, looking up occasionally as people came and went.

Half an hour later Ryan let her in, apologizing for the wait. She followed him into a conference room, where Detective Constable Sue Ziegler waited.

"Hello Jennifer, how are you?" Sue's voice and smile were warm, she was clearly happy to see her. Jennifer was equally pleased to see Sue, one of her former protection officers. She sensed from the setting and Sue's tone that this meeting was strictly on the record, so she refrained from small talk. They could catch up later.

"I am fine, thank you Detective Constable."

Sue gestured to the seat across at the head of the table and Jennifer sat. Detective Sergeant Gillespie sat across from Sue.

"This conversation will be on the record," Ryan said, clicking the recording device.

"Understood." Jennifer responded with a tiny nod.

"Let's start with what you observed as you walked to the grave earlier today. Did you see anyone?

"No."

"Was anything out of place, anything different?"

"Yes."

"Such as..." prompted Sue.

"The boards and straps were off to the side of the grave. Usually, they are in place. We don't always need a lowering device. When there's no family at the graveside it's not necessary. Normally I pull up, check the grave and, in this case, since the deceased was a John Doe, I would wait for the cemetery staff to assist."

"What time was this?"

"Exactly the minute? Can't say. I would suggest it was approximately 9:25 a.m."

The questions continued for twenty minutes, some repeated to ensure accuracy.

"Did you recognize the deceased?"

"Not immediately."

"Can you tell me, when you did recognize the deceased?" Another round of questions finally led to Jennifer identifying the body as Graham, the owner of Design A.

"How did you come to know him?"

"I hired his firm. He came with Carol, the other designer, to do the quote."

"Did Graham own a fuchsia measuring tape?"

"Not that I know of."

"Did you happen to notice if anyone in the firm owned a fuchsia measuring tape."

There it was. Carol was about to be implicated.

"Yes."

An hour later Jennifer was mentally exhausted and stiff from sitting. Determined not to let the questioning wear her down, she asked if she might stand and stretch.

Given permission, she stood beside her chair and stretched, then sat down again.

The conversation had turned to Carol and Jennifer's incident with Graham the day before. Detective Constable Ziegler started to direct the conversation to Carol and her interaction with Graham.

Jennifer began with her first visit to the design store, explained what she'd observed about Carol and Graham's relationship as partners. She admitted she had asked him to leave the funeral home and why. She hesitated when she remembered what Carol had said about leaving her alone. Sue didn't push. Jennifer hated to tell her, she didn't want Carol to look bad, but she had to be truthful.

Nearly three hours after entering the station the interview concluded.

Detective Sergeant Gillespie walked her to the door.

"Have you heard from the Crown Attorney's office yet?"

"No, I haven't. Why?"

"The preliminary hearing for Travis is coming up. While they have detailed reports from us, they may have some questions for you."

"Do I have to attend the hearing?"

"I don't think so. I suggested in my report that it might not be in your best interests and the Crown Attorney office is sensitive to victim impact. Travis will be there, of course. A few of the other individuals charged posted bail, including the officer you dealt with up north."

Jennifer felt a flash of fear. Ryan's information about Travis, the former interim funeral director who worked at Spencer Funeral Home before she took over, brought back uncomfortable memories. Her first thought when Ryan told her about the Crown Attorney was that she wanted to go back to her apartment, lock the door and sit and cuddle Grimsby.

It had been a different day than what she was used to: finding a body, being questioned for three hours, then having to think about the possibility of attending a preliminary hearing. She was glad she'd promised Marcia a visit. She missed her friend and confidant.

"Thank you for giving me a heads up on the preliminary hearing. I'm on my way to see Marcia. She insisted on making dinner."

Ryan grinned. "She's very stubborn. It's hard to get her to rest."

"I'll make sure she doesn't overdo it. See you later."

As she cleared the door of the station and walked to her car, she exhaled and inhaled deeply a few times in an attempt to relax. She checked in with Elaine, then drove to the falls and walked along the parkway, reviewing the murder and police interview over and over in her thoughts.

On the drive to Marcia's condo a while later, Jennifer still felt a tiny tug of discomfort. Nothing had been said to her about a possible suspect by either Detective, but the line of questioning focused on Carol. Had Carol been arrested at the funeral home? Maybe it was a good idea that she hadn't gone back.

8

Marcia hugged Jennifer gently as she greeted her at the door. Jennifer responded equally as carefully, not sure how much pain her friend was in. She cringed as she remembered that long afternoon sitting with a sick and unhappy Marcia.

"Mmm, that smells good," Jennifer said. The tempting scent of something cooking made her stomach growl.

"It's meatloaf and potatoes and veggies."

"Comfort food. I'm suddenly hungry. How are you?"

Marcia grinned. "I couldn't be better. I'm following orders and not overdoing things because I want to get back to work. If I mess up and overdo it, I have only myself to blame." Apart from being a bit pale, Marcia did look good.

"Let's see the ring. The suspense is killing me."

Marcia's smile lit up her face as she stuck out her left hand. Glistening in the light was a large oval-shaped faceted ruby set in gold, surrounded by scroll work and flanked by diamonds.

Jennifer gasped as she took her friend's hand. "Marcia—it's beautiful!"

"I know, right? It's not traditional. It's perfect. I love the Victorian look. I'll wear a wedding band at work, and this ring when I am not working. Don't you just love it?"

"I do, it suits you to a T. Wow."

"Ryan picked the perfect ring and setting. I don't know how he knew, but he got it right."

Marcia walked over to the kitchen counter. "Would you like a glass of wine with dinner?"

"Sounds good. Just half a glass though, I'm on call."

"White or red?"

"White, please."

"Then take a seat, I'll get your wine and our dinner and you can tell me what's happening at work."

Jennifer sat at the table wondering how to avoid discussing the situation evolving around Graham's death. She couldn't tell Marcia everything, and it would be hard. The two of them seldom kept secrets from each other. She glanced round the condo. It was cozy and modern. Marcia had a good eye when it came to decorating. She could focus on Marcia's health and the renovations, and avoid discussing the circumstances around Graham's death.

"Thanks for the basket," said Marcia as she prepared the plates. "I love what you guys picked out for me. You didn't have to."

"Yeah, we did. We love you. Glad you like it."

As the two of them started the meal, Jennifer brought Marcia up to speed about work.

"Brent hired a new director, he starts next week."

"He? That should balance us out nicely."

"His name is Gordon, he's been licensed for four years. He wants to get out of the Ottawa area. His girlfriend is a nurse and hopes to find work here too. This is delicious Marcia." Jennifer stopped talking long enough to finish her plate.

"You must have been hungry," laughed Marcia. "More?"

"Is Ryan going to be home for supper?"

"I set a plate aside for him, although he probably won't eat. He's working late."

"Yes please." Marcia had barely eaten. "Can't eat yet?" asked Jennifer, concerned for her friend.

"I can, but I'm not hungry. I nibbled throughout the day. How are the renovations coming along?"

"They may be completed by the time you come

back to work, except maybe for my kitchen upstairs. I haven't seen the furniture set up in the suite yet, it was delivered today."

"Busy day?"

Jennifer knew she couldn't talk about the murder. If Ryan felt it was appropriate he would give Marcia the details himself. She had to think fast.

"Lots of little things to catch up on. Ran a few errands, did a bit of shopping."

"Buy anything interesting?"

"No. Of course, I saw a few pairs of shoes you might like." Jennifer wasn't good with little white lies, but this time it went right over Marcia's head. Marcia loved shoes.

"Ryan says he'll build me a shoe closet. He says I have too many and it makes his OCD worse when they're scattered around."

"One can't have too many shoes," said Jennifer happily as she finished her second helping.

"No, I agree. Shoes are foot jewellery. Men don't get it. They wear the same pair over and over, day after day, except Phil of course." Phil was their funeral director friend from Toronto. Phil and his partner were fun to be around, they both loved to shop.

"Jeepers, you were hungry. I didn't make

dessert."

"I don't need dessert, I am full." Jennifer drained her wine glass and sat back in her chair, contented. The words were barely out of her mouth when her phone rang. She glanced down at it and took the information.

"Coroner's call." She looked at Marcia. "I gotta run." She hit the speed dial for Williams Funeral Home. Desta answered.

"Hi Desta, it's Jennifer. Is Jeff there?"

"No, he is doing a transfer. Brent is in."

"OK, thanks, put me through." Brent arranged to meet her at Spencer's and help with the coroner's call. He had a call too, but the family was coming in the morning.

"Sorry I can't help with the dishes," Jennifer said as she gave Marcia a quick hug. "Thanks a bunch for dinner."

"You're welcome!"

Jennifer hurried to the car and drove back to Spencer's funeral. When she pulled into the lot she spotted Brent's vehicle at the back. He had a key for Spencer's, and must have been inside because the lights were on in the front hall.

Brent opened the garage door as she approached. "I double-checked the supplies. Where are we off to?" he asked.

"A fire victim outside town." Jennifer punched the info into the GPS on her phone as Brent took the driver's seat.

"Fire scenes are tough," said Brent soberly, as he pulled out of the lot. "I remember when I was a kid, my uncle's house caught on fire and my cousin was killed. We lived close and watched the firemen put the fire out. My aunt was hysterical. The firemen couldn't get through the flames to save him. He was two years younger than me, only six. I still have nightmares about it."

"How awful. I can't imagine." They rode in silence, each lost in their own thoughts before Brent continued.

"Took a long time to get over the shock. I didn't want to go to school or outside to play. I cried over the slightest things. It was my first funeral. I remember the funeral director was so calm and kind. I saw tears in his eyes at the committal service. Fortunately, my mom saw the need to get me to a counsellor. It was several months after my cousin died before I started counselling."

Jennifer's phone interrupted their conversation. It was the answering service with a call on hold. Doug, the cemetery manager who'd risked his life to get Mr. Larson's casket into his garage, had died. Lori, Ronnie's wife called.

"Can you connect us please?" asked Jennifer. The answering service connected her to Lori's number.

"Lori? Jennifer Spencer. I am so, so, sorry to hear about Doug. You and Ronnie must be heartbroken.

"Yeah, Ronnie's taking it hard. We were wondering if you would take care of the funeral details."

"It would be my privilege."

"We called his sister, she doesn't want any fuss. She told us to go ahead with arrangements. Doug wanted burial. Of course, we'll bury him in the cemetery. He had a full-sized plot so his sister and her family could have their cremated remains buried with him. He did not like anything fancy or expensive."

"When can you and Ronnie meet with me?"

"Tomorrow morning maybe? I'll check with Ronnie. Let's try for nine."

"If you have any questions between now and when we meet, call me and ask the answering service to put you through."

"OK, thanks."

Jennifer disconnected and bit her lower lip, tears stinging her eyes. Doug had tried to rush ahead of the tornado to get the casket into a shelter. Why had he not hit the button on the lowering device? It would have exposed the casket to the rain but what difference would that had made? It was to be buried anyway.

Brent looked over at her. "Bad call?"

"Sad one, Doug, the cemetery manager, died. He never regained consciousness. I didn't get a chance to thank him for getting Mr. Larson's casket out of the storm."

Brent slowed as the fire trucks came into view. An officer was waiting and lifted the tape, another waved them closer to the scene.

A small bungalow had been destroyed by the fire, much of the structure gone. The air was heavy with the smell of smoke. A once pretty, well-kept garden had been trampled down by the hoses and firemen. Brent and Jennifer looked at each other.

"Ready?" asked Jennifer softly.

"Ready," said Brent, then took a deep breath in, exhaling slowly. As they exited the vehicle the fire chief approached Brent. Jennifer walked to the back of the van and pulled out a pair of work boots she kept stored there. She put her shoes on the floor of

131

the passenger side so she could change back as they drove to the hospital.

"You have a couple of options. The lady who died is in the kitchen at the side of the house. The structure is precarious." As Jennifer joined them, he walked them over to the shell of the house.

"If you go in carefully this way, the structure will hold, it has a full support beam underneath. Once you reach the victim, it's less stable. The other way is easier, from this side. He led them to the side of the house. "She's much closer, but that's where the structure is questionable."

Brent turned to Jennifer. "What do you think boss?" Once again Brent was gently letting another official know she was in charge.

"May I take a closer look?" she asked the fire chief.

"Yes ma'am," he responded. "Be careful." Jennifer skirted the edge of the structure, looked at both options, then turned to the chief.

"How old was this lady?" she asked.

"The neighbours said she was in her eighties."

She turned to Brent. "Let's use the two-man stretcher. I can take the short route myself, I'm smaller and lighter. Is that a viable option?" she asked the chief.

"It should work if you are cautious," he said.

Jennifer looked at Brent, who nodded. He went to the van and returned with the stretcher and supplies, helping her lay it out. She gloved and put on a protective gown.

"Be careful," he said quietly.

"I will."

Brent helped her step up onto the edge of the building, then handed her the stretcher.

Her heart was pounding a little as she inched her way across the remains of what was once a kitchen, brushing past a charred refrigerator. The body of the elderly lady was only a few feet into the house. She stood quietly for a few seconds. Even though she knew people usually succumb to smoke before fire, seeing a charred body was disturbing. It was a challenge to distinguish the body from the structure. She turned back to the fire crew.

"Can you tell me where the closest cross-beam is?"

One of the firemen ran his arm up and down. "This way." He stooped down to look in what was once the basement window. "About a foot to your left."

"Thank you," she responded. She placed the stretcher on the area of cross-beam, then crouched down and gently started to pry the body lose. Once or twice she stood to stretch. A slight shift of her foot caused it to displace the burned wood. She heard debris tumble to the basement below and slowly shifted her weight back. The process of preparing to move the body took over an hour before she was able to place the woman on the stretcher. She pulled her phone and used her flashlight to scan the area around the spot where the body had been. Usually, the firemen assisted with identifying body parts, this time with the structure unable to support them, she had to ensure she had completed the task. The yellow and red linoleum floor where the woman had been lying was the only colour around her, everything else was black.

"Brent, would you toss me the end of a rope, please? I think we might have to pull the stretcher across the floor to remove her. Then if the floor gives way, she's secured."

One of the firemen got a rake and cleared some of the burned debris by reaching over from the edge of the foundation. Brent tossed her the rope, she missed it the first time. It took several attempts. She was starting to feel a bit shaky from maintaining her position, afraid to move even a little bit.

She struggled to put the rope under the stretcher,

leaving enough at the top so she could lift it slightly as Brent pulled it out. She wound it around the handle at the bottom several times, knotted it, then again at the head—the part she would lift slightly as Brent pulled.

"Ready." Brent and one of the fireman pulled gently as Jennifer guided the stretcher off the beam and toward the men. Once or twice she heard material fall to the basement as she shifted her weight, causing her to hold her breath as the structure groaned and creaked.

It was with considerable relief she saw the stretcher reach the edge of the building. Retracing her path back the way she'd come in, a couple of firemen met her and lifted her down. She exhaled with relief.

"Thank you." As Brent and one of the firemen placed the stretcher in the van, on top of the regular transfer stretcher, she removed her blackened gloves and gown.

"I'll get rid of those for you ma'am," said one of the fireman. She handed them to him.

"I appreciate that. Thanks."

She turned to Brent. "Do you have the certificate?"

"Not yet, I forgot. I was busy watching."

"I forgot too," said the fire chief as he walked to his car and retrieved the death certificate the coroner had given him. He handed it to her. "Nice work."

"Thanks," she said as she climbed into the van. "I appreciate all your help."

Neither of them spoke until they were almost at the hospital. Brent broke the silence.

"You had me a little worried a couple of times, it was rather precarious." Jennifer started a bit when he spoke, she was thinking about Doug. She had been trying her best to put the fire scene out of her mind.

"It was a bit scary. That poor woman. That scene will haunt my dreams for a while."

As they pulled into the bay at the back of the hospital, she spoke again, "I was thinking, since Doug did so much to help with Mr. Larson and risking his life to get the casket out of the storm, what about doing a visitation and chapel service at no cost? I don't believe for one second that a person of his integrity and dedication should go un-mourned by the community."

"I think that's a great idea. I'd be happy to help with visitation and service. He was one of our colleagues. We could close Williams for the service and have all the staff attend, the answering service could cover."

"Then I'll discuss it with Ronnie and Lori." Brent watched while Jennifer opened the van doors and removed the fire victim. "I'll go to admitting and give them the certificate and get the key. I'll meet you at the morgue." He held the door for her as she pushed the stretcher through, then disappeared down the hall.

Jennifer stood outside the morgue door, hoping the air would help clear the strong smell of smoke from her clothing. She knew from past experience the scent would wash out of her clothes, but that olfactory déjà vu would assault her senses at random and the strong smell of smoke would cause her to relive the memory.

As she entered the back door of the hospital with the stretcher, no one was in sight. The pathology department was usually quiet, she seldom saw staff. Looking down at the stretcher and the outline of the woman she felt a rush of sadness.

Rather than fight it off she allowed herself to feel, knowing it was as much for Doug as for the victim of the fire. Doug would be riding back with her to the funeral home.

9

The first thing Jennifer did once she placed Doug in the prep room was to go to the suite. She barely recognized it. The new furniture and lighting added a softer, gentler ambience. She sat in all the chairs, looking at it from different angles before shutting down for the night.

Wondering if Carol would be working on the renovations, Jennifer rose early the next morning and went looking for her. One of the tradespeople who had the key, let the others in and they were hard at work. The main floor would be completed in a few days at the rate they were going. There was no sign of Carol or Agnes.

She went up to one of the carpenters who was placing the baseboard around the perimeter of the wall and asked him if he'd seen either woman. He looked up from his task and shook his head no. She felt a tiny twinge of concern for Carol. Had she been arrested?

On her way to her office she paused to pour

herself a coffee before sitting quietly for a few minutes. Where was Carol? She pulled her phone and checked her email and messages. Not a word. There was nothing from Agnes either.

Having dinner with Marcia had lifted her spirit, and Jennifer recognized how much the two of them depended on each other for emotional support. Brent had helped fill that void too, and she realized it had been mutual. She dialed Williams. Desta answered on the second ring.

"Hi Desta, how are things?" They chatted for a few minutes, Desta informed her that Graham's visitation and service were to be at Williams. Brent had taken the call when they returned from the coroner's call the night before. Desta put her through to him.

"Hi again!" she said cheerfully. "Desta tells me you will be doing Graham's service. By any chance did Carol call you?"

"No, it was his sister. She wanted to have the service here, where Graham's friends are. Any sign of Carol?"

"Nope, or Agnes."

"That can't be good, I wonder if the police have arrested Carol or are questioning either of them?" Brent wondered.

"I was wondering the same thing. If you need me, call. I can give you a hand."

"Thanks. Vice versa."

She had barely disconnected when the funeral home line rang again. She was a little surprised when the caller introduced himself.

"Ms. Spencer, it's David from the news station. We met when I was working with the newspaper?"

"Of course, how are you David? What can I do for you?"

She was a bit puzzled by his call, then decided he was probably looking for information about funerals or something related to them.

"I received an anonymous tip earlier today that your funeral home had something to do with a murder?"

"What?" She was stunned.

"A designer was murdered. We covered the story last night. The caller suggested it involved your funeral home."

"I appreciate you calling, David. Yes, I saw the story on the news last night. I haven't got anything to say other than his firm, Design A, is doing some renovations here. Perhaps the police could help you?" She knew he wouldn't accept that answer, it was his job to get the story.

"So you deny that your firm is under investigation and that the Board of Funeral Service has cited you for violations?"

"Is that what the caller told you?" She was starting to get angry. Her face grew warm and her heart rate accelerated. She took a deep breath in and out. *Keep it together, he's just doing his job.*

"My source suggested that your firm was trying to silence the designer for reporting you."

"Any violation of the Act is a matter of public record. Contact the Board of Funeral Services. They will answer that question. I can assure you that I am not aware of any reports of violations for either funeral home."

"Is any of your staff a suspect in the designer's murder?"

Jennifer's jaw clenched. "Not that I am aware of. That is a police matter and you would have to ask the Homicide Division." She took a deep breath. Her mind raced; she needed to calm down. "Can you tell me about the caller?"

David hesitated before answering. She figured he had to protect his source, but at the same time, it was an anonymous tip. She needed to confirm her suspicions.

"It was a man. He refused to identify himself.

He stated that the designer was murdered because he was going to report violations. It's a stretch, so I did look up your firm on the Board website—your record is perfect and you've passed all inspections. I just needed to confirm it with you."

"Thank you, David. I appreciate the heads up."

"It was odd, don't you think? That the body was found in a grave that *your* funeral home had ordered opened?"

Jennifer cringed. She had to answer honestly and if she refused to comment it might look worse than just telling the truth. She started dialing the alternate funeral home line on her cellphone.

"I agree. It was odd." The line started ringing.

"If there is nothing else, I have to grab that call. Thanks, David."

"Bye, Ms. Spencer."

She tapped off, silenced the second ring she'd triggered and sat back in her chair. *Alymer or Elmer? It had to be one of them. How dare they!* She slammed her hand a little too hard on her desk.

"Ow!" she yelped. *Serves you right for being so dramatic. Don't let the Larson's drag you down. Let it go. It was good of David to let you know.*

Feeling a little restless and a bit angry, Jennifer sought out Elaine when she arrived at nine, and gave her the details of the coroner's call, Doug's death and her idea that Spencer's could do his funeral service. Elaine was in full agreement. She'd spoken with Doug over the years and was fond of him. Jennifer chose not to mention the reporter's phone call.

"Your Uncle Bill and Doug had a great friendship. Hard to believe they're both gone now." She looked at Jennifer closely. "According to the death certificate he had untreated hypertension, he could have had that stroke at any time."

"But it wasn't any time, he had it as a result of struggling to get Mr. Larson to a safe place ahead of, or possibly during, a tornado. He did it all by himself."

"Jennifer, this may sound cruel, but I believe you would be the first to caution your staff in similar circumstances." Elaine's serious tone made her more attentive. "Mr. Larson was already dead. Doug should have left him on the grave and taken shelter himself. He risked his life for a dead person. Admirable in one way, but not sensible. You and Marcia and Jeff did the right thing. The warning was out for a good reason and you heeded it. Had you stayed in the cemetery in the path of the tornado you all could have been killed."

Jennifer nodded soberly. Elaine was correct, taking life-threatening risks for a deceased person made no sense.

"You're right. The main thing now is to ensure Doug's friends can meet together to grieve, and this is what I can offer them." She turned to leave, then remembered why she had sought out Elaine.

"Oh—one more thing. Did you hear from Carol or Agnes this morning?"

Elaine shook her head.

"I hope Carol hasn't been arrested."

"I'm sure Agnes can complete the renovations, she's more than capable," responded Elaine reassuringly.

"I'm sure she can, that's not what bothers me. I don't for one minute think Carol killed Doug. Whoever did, though, covered their tracks well."

"Like I said before, Graham was not a nice person," Elaine said pragmatically. "He tormented Carol. Maybe she did kill him. Everyone has a breaking point."

They were interrupted by the arrival of Ronnie and Lori. Elaine and Jennifer greeted them, and they chatted for a while before Jennifer took over the front office to make the arrangements. Ronnie looked drained and tired in his grief for his friend.

Both of them were surprised when Jennifer suggested she would do a visitation and service for Doug. They spent the next few hours planning it. Ronnie called Doug's sister, who agreed to fly in for the service.

It wasn't until late-afternoon when Jennifer had finished prepping Doug before Agnes came into the funeral home, looking discouraged—her face drawn and sad. Not wanting to interfere or stress her out, Jennifer refrained from approaching her other than to say *hi* in passing on her way up to her apartment for a late lunch. Agnes mumbled a response back.

It was after five o'clock before Agnes did approach her, tapping timidly on her office door jam. Jennifer looked up at her stricken face.

"Come in Agnes, take a seat."

Agnes sat, head down, looking at her hands knotted in her lap. A tear ran down her cheek as she attempted to get the words out, "Graham was murdered and Carol has been arrested. I don't know what to do."

"I'm so sorry about Graham."

"They think Carol killed him." Agnes kept her head down, her hands now busy in her lap as she rubbed them over and over.

"Do you think Carol murdered Graham?"

145

Jennifer asked that question as gently as she could, she could tell the poor woman was distraught.

"They kept asking me about Carol. They have evidence."

"What evidence?"

"Her measuring tape was...was..." Agnes broke into a flood of tears.

Choosing to give Agnes time to calm down and to see what she knew, Jennifer sat waiting.

"Her measuring tape was around Graham's neck."

Feigning ignorance and feeling a bit guilty for discussing the murder, Jennifer raised an eyebrow. "How do they know it was Carol's tape? Fingerprints?"

"It's pink. She was the only one of us who had a pink measuring tape."

"Then her fingerprints would be all over it," said Jennifer quietly. Agnes had avoided answering her question about whether or not she thought Carol had killed Graham.

"Why would Carol want Graham dead?"

Agnes finally looked at Jennifer, her eyes puffy and red. "Carol hated him. He loved her, and she treated him like he was dirt."

Jennifer was a bit taken aback by that statement.

Graham had not appeared to love Carol at all, it seemed to be a work relationship that wasn't strong on mutual respect.

Agnes continued, "I can complete the renovations, the plans are in place, if that is OK with you."

"It's more than OK, I would appreciate it. I need to get the funeral home finished and the lounge and offices up and running."

"What about the kitchen?"

"Are you able to oversee and manage it?"

Agnes seemed to change over a few seconds. She sat taller and morphed from her mousy demeanour into one of a confident professional.

"I don't have a degree in design but I do have first-hand experience. I can do it. Carol would not want to let you down."

"I'm pleased to hear that." Jennifer smiled at her. "When do you think the downstairs will be completed?"

"Early next week," confirmed the newly self-assured Agnes. She stood and looked down at Jennifer.

"I'll be here in the morning." With that, she turned and left the office.

Checking the time, Jennifer rose, made sure the

garage door was locked and went to lock the front door. She watched as smiling Agnes drove out of the parking lot.

Agnes is an Eliza Doolittle. Given a chance to shine, it looks like she'll do just that.

Jennifer locked up and went upstairs for supper. Grimsby, happy to see her, dropped his squeaky toy at her feet. She laughed as he chased up and down the furniture as she threw it for him. Finally spent, he left it on the chair and curled up in her arms, purring contentedly.

Reflecting over the events of the day, Jennifer was jolted out of her contemplation by her phone. The number showed unknown. *Telemarketer probably.* She had to answer it, it could be a first call. Annoyed that her train of thought had been interrupted, she was a bit abrupt as she hit the button.

"Spencer Funeral Home, Jennifer speaking." She realized her tone of voice reflected her annoyance and she cringed slightly when she heard the caller's voice.

"Jennifer, it's Carol. I don't have much time on the phone. I have to see you." Jennifer was shocked to hear her voice, she sounded tired and defeated.

"Carol, how are you? I can't talk to you about Graham, I am not allowed to."

148

"I'm OK. I didn't do it." There was silence on the line. Likely Carol thought about Jennifer's words. "I understand you can't talk to me, but can you talk to my sister Penny, at least hear her out? I want her to tell you what happened. She'll come and see you tomorrow."

"All right." Jennifer heard a soft click as she hung up. Her mind raced. Carol would not have been arrested if Detective Sergeant Gillespie didn't have solid evidence.

She sat with the still-purring Grimsby in her arms, wrestling with the situation. *I am missing something. What is it? I'm not supposed to talk to anyone about this. I'll have to let Carol's sister do the talking.* She knew that kind of rationalization would not sit well with Detective Sergeant Gillespie, but figured if he didn't know it wouldn't matter.

Tired and a bit edgy, she had a bath and went to bed early. Unable to concentrate long enough to read, she put her book down and turned out the light. Sleep eluded her, and as the hours ticked by she was no closer to understanding what she might have missed that caused Carol to be charged with murder.

Agnes arrived at the funeral home promptly at 9:00 a.m. The workmen were talking about one of

149

the carpenters who'd been questioned about Graham's murder. Jennifer pulled Agnes aside.

"What's all that about?"

"Apparently one of the guys had a big fight with Graham the day before he died. He told his crew that the police suspect he helped Carol kill him." She shook her head. "I can't see him doing that, he's a nice guy."

"Did he get arrested too?"

Agnes shrugged. "I don't know. Maybe. He's not here. We can still stay on schedule without him." Agnes excused herself and went to check something with one of the carpenters.

Maybe that worker did help carry the body to the grave, which explains why there were no drag marks from the road.

She poured herself a coffee and took it into her office. The glass wall was in place, dulling the noise of the saws and hammers. She completed the file for Doug's service, checked the obituary listing online and started getting a personnel file ready for Gordon, the new funeral director.

"Boo!" She jumped as Marcia poked her head around the corner, laughing.

"Oh, my gosh, what are you doing here? Shouldn't you be resting?" Jennifer got to her feet and hugged her friend.

"I thought I'd hang out for a few hours, if that's OK. I'm allowed out as long as I don't overdo it."

"Good, have a seat, we can catch up. Do you want tea or coffee?"

"Tea sounds perfect."

Jennifer prepared the tea and put it on her desk in front of Marcia.

"I like the way the renovations are going." Marcia picked up her cup and took a sip.

"Me too. It'll be great to have the extra workspace for you and other staff. I was getting a personnel file ready for Gordon, he starts next week."

"What else is new?"

Jennifer thought for a second, then started to laugh. "I completely forgot to tell you about Mr. Whitney. Brent set him up beautifully."

"Oh, do tell. This sounds delicious." Jennifer rose and closed the office door. Marcia and Jennifer had a good laugh at Mr. Whitney's expense. As Jennifer wiped the tears of laughter from her eyes, she told Marcia that Brent was quite prepared to do it again if the situation warranted it. The laughter released some of Jennifer's unease about Graham's death. It was good to have Marcia back.

"Did Ryan tell you why he was working late the night we had dinner?" asked Jennifer.

"He did. He figured I should know before I came here."

"I can't discuss it, but at least you're aware of the situation. Agnes has taken over the renovations."

They dropped the subject and talked about employee training and how the changes at Williams would make all their lives easier. Marcia suggested the restaurant for Gordon's welcome dinner and offered to take over the arrangements.

Several hours later Marcia rose to leave. "I'll be back for Doug's service tomorrow. Are you expecting a crowd?"

"Not sure, I know Ronnie and Lori made some calls."

"I'll be here at ten. I can't wait to give Ryan the details about Mr. Whitney's response when he found out you're the owner. Ryan will love it."

Feeling lighter in spirit than she had for a while, Jennifer found the rest of the day flew by. She took a couple of inquiries about the cost of services and set up an appointment with one of the families for the next afternoon.

Before she knew it, Elaine had said goodnight and Agnes and the workmen had left. As she locked up the funeral home and went upstairs for supper when her phone rang.

"Spencer Funeral Home, Jennifer speaking." She made sure she didn't sound annoyed or tired, she was embarrassed after doing so the day before.

"My name is Penny. I'm Carol's sister. When can we talk?"

"When are you free?"

"In about an hour?"

"Could we meet at Tim Horton's on Main?"

"Sure. Carol gave me a description of you, I'm sure I'll find you. I have blonde hair, glasses and I'm wearing a green sweatshirt, jeans and a grey ski jacket."

"Sound's good, see you then."

I will ask you not to discuss the case with anyone. Jennifer ignored DS Gillespie's voice in her head. She wasn't going to talk about Carol's case with Penny, she was going to sit back and listen to what Penny had to say.

Arriving at the always busy coffee shop, Jennifer took a seat at a small table near the window and watched the entrances. It wasn't hard to spot Carol's sister, they could have been twins. Jennifer rose to greet her.

153

"I'm Jennifer, you must be Penny."

Penny tentatively shook her hand. Her face was etched with fatigue.

"Come, sit. You look tired."

"You have no idea, this has been a nightmare."

Jennifer got tea for both of them and set the mug in front of Penny, who was staring dully out the window into the darkness.

"I have to tell you, I'm not allowed to discuss the case with anyone," she said. "However, I'm fond of Carol and I will listen to what you have to say."

"Anything to get my sister free. She didn't do it. She was set up or something." Penny's eyes brimmed with tears. She picked up her mug and wrapped her hands around it. She hadn't taken her winter coat off.

"How can you stand this damp cold? I wonder why Carol moved to the Niagara region, the humidity here is dreadful." She shivered.

Jennifer smiled. "That part can be hard to get used to. But the Niagara region is amazing with the vineyards and the canal and the falls."

"I know you're usually busy, Carol was telling me about your funeral home. Let me get right to the point. Carol couldn't have killed Graham. After work, she was with a... um...a friend."

Jennifer cocked her head.

"He's married and he's well-known in the area. They spent the night together."

"Then she has an alibi."

Penny's shoulders slumped. "No. Carol doesn't want him identified."

Jennifer looked at Penny intensely. "So, Carol is willing to spend years in prison for him? That makes no sense."

"It's worse than that. He'll deny he knew her. Carol said they'd been seeing each other for several months."

Forgetting that she wasn't going to get involved, Jennifer threw caution to the winds.

"Get his DNA. Something he touched must be in Carol's possession. That will prove he's lying. Getting him to admit she was with him should be easy after that."

"She won't listen to me. I agree with you. I don't care who he is either. She needs to tell me his name. I'll confront him. I'll do what it takes to see her go free. I know my sister didn't do it."

"What about Graham? What kind of relationship did Graham and Carol have?"

Penny snorted, the derision in her voice obvious. "He took her for every cent she had. He lured her

155

into his Toronto business, a business that he drove into the ground with the swanky parties and drug habit and then, when that failed, dragged her down here. She's the brains behind the business, the talent. He was nothing. He took her money and used it for drugs. I warned her."

"Maybe she thought she could help him?"

Penny rolled her eyes. "I think almost every woman thinks they can change their boyfriend or spouse, or in this case, co-worker. I did the same with my husband. Now I'm divorced. My grandmother, God rest her soul, used to say all the time that 'we can't change other people, we can only change ourselves.'"

Jennifer thought back to her relationships and nodded. "I thought my first boyfriend would change too." But she quickly changed the subject, as she was more interested in Carol's arrest, not her relationships. "What does her lawyer say?"

"She hasn't met with one yet. She was appointed one and has a meeting pending. They talked on the phone briefly. She told her not to talk to police anymore until they meet."

"Do you have any idea who might have set her up?"

"I was hoping you would know." Penny sighed.

"One of the workmen was interviewed, he and Graham had a row apparently."

"Carol said the police thought he might have been an accomplice. Apparently, he had an alibi."

"Have you spoken to the police yet?"

"No," responded Penny. "What good what that do?"

"Tell Detective Constable Ziegler what you told me. What have you got to lose? If Carol won't help herself, and she asked you to help, how else can you help her?"

Penny looked at her intensely. "You really do sound like my grandmother. Pragmatic. Too bad Carol doesn't carry that DNA."

"She's an artist." Jennifer smiled as she said that. She was aware that she sounded like Anne, her twin. Anne's reporter brain was usually stuck on "just the facts and meet the deadline."

"You're right. I didn't come all this way to sit on my hands. I'll get in touch with the police." She drained the last of her tea and stood. "Thanks."

"Good luck. Remember, we didn't have this conversation." Jennifer felt a pang of guilt, she wouldn't talk about the murder with Marcia but she would with a complete stranger?

Penny gave her a faint smile and walked away,

this time looking the part of a woman on a mission.

10

Ronnie and Lori arrived with Doug's sister an hour before the service. After introductions, Jennifer led them to the lounge where Marcia was getting ready for the post-funeral reception. The chapel was set up for the service, a few bouquets of flowers around the casket adding a touch of colour.

"Look what I found," said Ronnie. He pulled out his phone and showed Jennifer a picture of a small, weathered statue of Jesus and Mary. Jennifer looked at Ronnie, puzzled.

"Doug was Catholic, he never missed a mass. Not too many people knew that about him. He also had a love of graveyards and, when he could, he would purchase old grave decorations and use them for indigent graves or families who couldn't afford extras. He was a bit of a softie that way." For a moment Ronnie looked off into space as he remembered his friend. "Anyway, he salvaged this statue from a grave that a family was updating. He loved this piece. I found it in the back of his garage covered with an old sheet. He was saving it for someone special."

"Ronnie is going to put it on his stone." Lori stood beside Ronnie and took his arm.

"Yeah. Least I could do." He looked down at his wife and patted her hand. He looked at Jennifer. "The grave is ready."

"So is the funeral coach. I thought you might like to take him after the reception. I know we agreed to do the committal in the chapel and take Doug to the cemetery later. We can go after the reception. I'll ride with you and bring the coach back."

Ronnie cleared his throat, tears threatening to spill. "Thanks. I thought you would bring him in the van, which is perfectly fine, the hearse seems more dignified."

"Have you met with the celebrant yet?"

"No, the priest should be here soon though." Jennifer had noticed that Marcia raised an eyebrow as soon as she heard Ronnie mention *priest*. She had not been aware Doug was Catholic, she should have asked. Marcia quickly disappeared.

"Then let's go to the chapel and see if there's anything you'd like changed."

Jennifer led the way to the chapel door then

stood back as Doug's sister and Ronnie and Lori entered, still arm in arm. She wasn't surprised to see Marcia setting up the prayer rail and candles. Marcia stepped back, surveyed her work and left by the side door. Lori looked back at Jennifer and nodded. She closed the back doors to give them the time they needed.

Ten minutes later the priest arrived. He was a pleasant young man and after giving him his honorarium, Jennifer directed him into the chapel to speak with Ronnie and Lori. Brent came in from the garage, followed by Desta and Jeff—everyone congregating in the lounge for coffee. Marcia came out into the lobby to find Jennifer.

"I forgot to tell you, Ryan will be coming with another officer."

"Did Ryan know Doug?" Jennifer was puzzled, she doubted their paths would have crossed.

Marcia's face was mischievous. "No, but the Constable coming with him made his acquaintance. You'll see."

"Thank you for moving so quickly with the Catholic setup, I didn't realize Doug was Catholic and the celebrant was going to be a priest."

"No problem. I'll print off some prayer cards."

A few minutes late Mr. Whitney came in,

followed by some of his staff. Jennifer greeted them as Ronnie, Lori and the priest came out of the chapel. Jennifer made the introductions. She was pleased that Mr. Whitney, who ran the largest cemetery in the area, had taken the time to honour one of his colleagues. More and more people arrived: funeral directors from the district, municipal officials, and other cemetery managers from the region. Ryan showed up with Constable Ayers. As Ronnie shook the young man's hand, Jennifer moved closer to eavesdrop.

"I'm sorry about your friend," said Constable Ayers.

"Thank you," responded Ronnie sincerely. He caught Jennifer's eye and nodded, pleased that Ryan had brought the young constable to Doug's funeral.

"Good for Ryan. Constable Ayers didn't handle the call well," she said in a low voice to Marcia.

"Ryan thought it might be good training for Constable Ayers to attend a funeral, so he asked the Staff Sergeant if he could bring him. He's new to the force and has a few things to learn," responded Marcia. "I'm proud of Ryan, he could have talked to him about his attitude. Instead, he brought him here on a field trip, sort of, and educated him. Ryan said it's Ayers' first funeral."

By the time the service started the one hundred fifty seat chapel was nearly full. Jennifer handed Marcia the committal sand, then took a seat at the back of the chapel, ready to cue the music before the benediction.

Her mind wandered a bit during the service. She was surprised at the number of people who'd come to honour Doug, most of them in the funeral industry in one way or another. Her thoughts drifted into how the construction was going. She was pleased the renovations were almost over. Agnes had made sure the area was clean near the lounge for the reception. The workers would be back this afternoon to finish up. The upstairs apartment renovations would start tomorrow. She was so lost in thought she nearly missed the cue to play Ave Maria.

She slipped out the door as the music started and double-checked the lounge. The door to the selection room was open a crack and she could hear voices on the other side.

Peeking through she saw Agnes and one of the workmen, the same one the police had questioned. They were deep in conversation. Agnes handed him a small package, he handed her some money. Jennifer watched quietly, barely breathing. Agnes wasn't saying much; the workman was appeared to be doing most of the talking. She caught a few snatches of the conversation, 'wife' being the most prominent. The sound of voices caused Jennifer to back away as the service ended and people started to enter the lounge. She quietly closed the door, afraid they might see her. She made a mental note to discuss it with Marcia later.

Greeting some of the guests, she went back to the lobby to say goodbye to the people who were not staying for the reception. Not many people left after the service, it wasn't every day that funeral personnel were able to get together. And people were eager to chat. Even Ryan and Constable Ayers stayed for a few minutes. Ryan introduced him to some of the directors and cemetery managers.

It was a busy few hours as people ate and socialized. Jennifer kept an eye on Marcia, warning her once or twice not to overdo it.

"Why don't you mingle and get to know some of the funeral directors we haven't met yet. It's been a long day for you."

"It has gone by quickly. It's good to be back at work. You're such a mother hen, thanks for watching out for me."

By late afternoon Ronnie and Lori were the only

ones left. With Ronnie and Brent and Elaine's help they loaded the casket into the funeral coach. Jennifer sat beside Ronnie as he drove, Lori following behind in their car. Jennifer and Lori watched as Ronnie completed the interment and filled in the grave. It was a solemn moment for the three of them.

As she said her goodbyes, and pulled out of the cemetery, her phone vibrated. She stopped on the side of the road to check. Marcia had a texted to notify her a family had walked in to make an arrangement, and she would take care of it.

Jennifer took her time driving the funeral coach to Williams, where she sought out Brent after arriving.

"There were a few more people at the service than I expected," she said to him.

"Doug was well-respected in the area. I had a chance to talk with many of the other funeral home owners. It was a great opportunity to meet them, it isn't often we have time. Some of them were a little curious about you, they knew you owned both funeral homes."

Even though she was interested to know what might have been said about her, she let it drop. It wasn't important. "Well, I'm glad we were able to do something for Doug. Marcia's with a family right now, is Jeff free to run me back to Spencer's?"

"He should be."

"Thanks for your help today."

With Brent's cheery, "You're welcome," she left his office to find Jeff.

Marcia was still with the family when she got back to Spencer's. It was after five o'clock. Elaine was in the lounge finishing the cleanup.

"There isn't much food left, but I made up three 'care' packages for you, Marcia and I."

Jennifer looked around the tidy lounge. "Thank you. I'm really tired. It feels later than it is. This should take care of supper."

"I'll see you tomorrow." Elaine disappeared into the front office and left a few minutes later.

Jennifer made herself a tea and started to nibble on a sandwich. She was hungry, she hadn't taken the time for lunch and she had not eaten during the reception.

She heard Marcia walk the family out and waited a few minutes before she found her in the front office.

"Are you feeling OK?"

"I feel great." Marcia filled Jennifer in on the details of the call.

"I'll do the transfer tomorrow. In the meantime, though, I wanted to run something past you." She told Marcia about the incident with Agnes and the workman.

"Maybe she sold him some weed," suggested Marcia.

"Agnes doesn't seem the type to do pot, let alone deal—although I thought I heard him say something about his wife."

"There's a type?" Marcia's eyebrows were raised. "Maybe his wife is ill, but goodness Jen, lots of 'normal' people do pot. I used some post-op."

"Seriously?"

Marcia laughed. "I seldom use it, but my neighbour got some for me."

Jennifer's jaw dropped.

"You are such an old soul." Marcia smiled. "My doctor suggested it. Narcotics make me sick and I won't take them."

"I guess I am a bit old fashioned. And a bit out of touch."

"It's a matter of time before it is legalized," Marcia added. She quickly changed the subject. "Are they starting the renovations upstairs tomorrow?"

"Apparently. Grimsby isn't going to be amused."

"You and Grimsby can stay with me if it gets to be too much for him. Or you," she added quickly. Marcia and Grimsby were great friends.

"Thanks. I'll keep that in mind. In the meantime, I think I'll go down to the falls for a while. It's a nice evening and I feel the need to stare at the water for a bit. Elaine left a plate of leftovers in the lounge for you."

"I'm almost done with the initial file set-up," Marcia said. "I'll lock up. I can take calls for you for the next five or six hours. You haven't had much of a break."

"I'd appreciate it." Jennifer sighed. She was intrinsically weary, she felt as if she could sleep for days. "The walk will be good for my soul."

Marcia chuckled. "In that case, goodbye you dear old soul."

Jennifer took her sandwiches upstairs, changed into her jeans and a sweatshirt and, after ensuring Grimsby had clean water and food, she slipped out the garage door.

Jennifer liked mingling incognito with the tourists at the falls. Finding a spot on the wall, she sat on the edge and watched the water rush over the precipice. As darkness deepened and the falls were

168

lit by the LED lights, Jennifer continued to revel in the mist from the cascading water and the cool air. Eventually, as the crowds thinned she went into the welcome centre at Table Rock and got herself a tea at Tim Horton's. Finding a quiet table at the window she sat enjoying the changing lights on the falls. Her phone interrupted her. It was Penny, who got right to the point.

"Hi Jennifer. I did as you suggested. Detective Constable Ziegler listened to what I had to say. Without the name of the guy Carol was seeing though, she didn't offer much hope. So, I went over to Carol's apartment and guess what I found?"

"His name?"

"Nope, his tie. I'm going to take it back to DC Ziegler and ask if she'll check for DNA or at least ask Carol who owns it. I have to fly back home for work tomorrow, so I thought I'd let you know."

"How is Carol?"

"Still stubborn. She seems to think the police will find the real killer. She knows what she's being charged with. She knows the consequences. She can't make bail, I can't make bail for her, and she still won't give up his name."

"It's almost like she is guilty," suggested Jennifer.

"Exactly, except she didn't do it. I know my sister. She has bad taste in partners, but she isn't a killer."

"Maybe a court appearance will jolt her into reality."

"Something has to. She's not a stupid person, but she sure is blind to her current situation. She needs a wake-up call."

"Keep me posted. Have a safe trip home."

"Night Jennifer."

Jennifer sat and stared at the falls for another hour before heading back to her apartment. Looking at the water rush and tumble was cleansing. She was relaxed and lazy.

Back home, she watched TV for an hour before crawling into bed, Grimsby curled up at her feet.

The rest of the week passed quickly, with three new calls. Renovations had begun in the apartment. Poor Grimsby was beside himself with the kerfuffle and Marcia insisted on taking him until it was over. Jennifer decided to stay in her apartment, the evenings and nights were quiet and she preferred to be readily available for coroner's calls. She felt lost without her cat in his spot on the top of the couch and at the foot of her bed at night, and had trouble sleeping. But she knew Grimsby was less stressed with Marcia. The better part of her weekend was spent at Williams helping with their services. With Christmas coming, and influenza season building, there was an increase in death calls. The weekend passed quickly, Jennifer had no time to dwell on Carol's situation.

Monday morning, as they were having coffee in lounge, Elaine took a call in Jennifer's office. She heard Elaine mention that she was sure the directors would be delighted to help. As Elaine placed the caller on hold, she turned to Jennifer.

"It's the vice-principal at Niagara Secondary. One of the presenters for career day has taken ill and they wondered if you'd be able to step in and do a short presentation."

"When?"

"This afternoon."

Jennifer looked at Elaine incredulously.

"You can do it, take Marcia. I suspect it'll be fun. Here." She handed Jennifer the phone.

"What's the VP's name?"

"Ms. Saunders."

Taking a deep breath, Jennifer watched Elaine take the call off hold.

"Ms. Saunders, Jennifer Spencer. I understand

you had a cancellation for career day?"

"We did. I know it's short notice, but one of my colleagues told me about your talk at the public school and we would appreciate your help."

"I think my staff and I will be able to step in. How long is the presentation?"

"With a short talk and a Q & A, maybe 20 minutes?"

After confirming the time, Jennifer hung up. "Public school kids are one thing, teenagers are another," she said to Elaine.

"Teenagers are another what?" asked Marcia as she entered the lounge.

Jennifer turned to her and flashed her sweetest smile. "You and I are doing a career day presentation at the high school this afternoon."

"What? How did that happen?"

"2:00 p.m., we meet with the vice-principal at 1:30. It's Elaine's fault."

Elaine laughed. "Don't blame me, I just answered the phone. You two make a great team, it'll be fun."

"It might be kind of fun," Marcia said. "Speaking of fun, that reminds me, I have to stop and pick up some more cat treats. We can do that on the way back."

"More treats? I gave you a full bag. Grimsby will get fat."

"Tell that to Ryan. He has Grimsby doing tricks for treats. The two of them play half the evening. Come on, let's discuss our talk over coffee."

At 1:25 sharp Jennifer and Marcia pulled up to the high school. Marcia broke the silence as they walked to the front door.

"The last time I paid this much attention to my appearance was the day we fired Drew and Stephanie."

Jennifer held the door for Marcia. "You were brilliant that day. I was in awe. I couldn't have done it."

"This time I drew a page from your playbook. Remember how you told me if you tell yourself you're the expert you can act and appear confident? More or less?"

"So you're not nervous?"

"A little. But it's only twenty minutes and I bet not too many students know what we do with our day. They probably think dead bodies are gross and zombies exist."

After meeting the vice-principal, they were escorted to the gym. Throughout the hallways were booths and tables for colleges and universities, businesses and employment agencies. The VP led them through the back door of the stage. They stood in the wings and watched a financial planner talk about the importance of investing. As he droned on and on, Marcia stifled a yawn. He left the stage to polite applause.

"Our next speaker scheduled was a journalist, but he has taken ill. Instead, we have two funeral directors, Ms. Spencer and Ms. McGovern who have agreed to step in at the last moment. Let's welcome them."

Jennifer and Marcia walked onto the stage of the large auditorium. The students were all talking at once and they could hear words like undertaker, dead people and zombie from the floor.

Marcia stepped up first. The room quieted down quickly. Opening with 'I see dead people' (a line from one of her favourite movies), she had them laughing and twenty minutes later, Jennifer wound up their presentation on a sober note. They left to a thunderous round of applause.

Walking back to the car, Marcia announced they should go to the mall. "This calls for a new pair of shoes."

Jennifer laughed. "Sure, I'm all wound up

anyway." She called Elaine, gave her the details and, once assured it was quiet at the funeral home, the two of them spent the next couple of hours window shopping. Marcia did find a pair of shoes and a purse, both red.

"I'm going to stop at the washroom while you get the cat treats. Here." She handed Marcia some money.

"I got this," Marcia protested.

"No, I insist."

"No, no, *I* insist." They laughed at each other's silliness as Marcia finally took the money.

As Jennifer washed her hands in the ladies' room, a teenager approached her. "I enjoyed yours and your friend's talk at school today," she said shyly. Jennifer turned to her.

"Thank you," she said sincerely. "Have you decided what you want to do when you finish school?"

The young woman hung her head. "I want to go to university and study to become a therapist but..." Her voice trailed off.

"But what?" Jennifer prompted.

"I don't think I can do it. It's hard."

Jennifer studied her demeanour. Her body language alone showed a lack of confidence, her head was still down. "What are you finding hard about it?"

She took her time answering. "There are students who are much smarter than me. I applied to go to Queen's University, but I don't think I'll get in."

"There were students much smarter than me in funeral service education too. I was sure I wouldn't get in. I did get accepted and I struggled for every mark. I didn't make the top ten percent, I was somewhere in the middle. Do you know what one of the professor's told me?"

The teen remained silent and shook her head.

"That 'C' students who work diligently and do their best, make the best employees. That's because they had to work twice as hard to get there and they valued their opportunity."

This time she looked at Jennifer with a spark of interest.

"Come, stand beside me," Jennifer said. She moved the young woman to the mirror. "There is always, always, going to be somebody smarter than you, or funnier, or more social. That's just the way it is. Look at yourself closely." The young woman stared at her reflection in the mirror. "There is your competition. The only person you need to compete with is yourself."

"That makes sense," the young woman said, after staring at her reflection closely.

"I look for several things in an employee. Attitude and work ethic are the most important. Are they a team player? Do they work well with others? Are they willing to learn new skills? Are they honest? I couldn't care less about their marks in school."

"Thank you," said the young woman softly. "I never looked at it that way before." She smiled at Jennifer. "I have to run, I'll be late for work." Jennifer watched her scurry through the door.

Jennifer met Marcia outside the dollar store and told her about the encounter.

"You and I learned the hard way, didn't we?" Marcia said. "I mean, you were on your own before you finished high school, me too. Sometimes I think we were the lucky ones. We grew up fast."

"It wasn't easy. There were times I wanted to give up. I have Uncle Bill and Aunt Jean to thank. But here we are now, older and wiser."

"Who are you calling *old?*" Marcia scolded.

Marcia's phone interrupted their reminiscence. She glanced down at it and pumped her fist. "Yes!"

She turned to Jennifer. "What are you doing Friday?"

"Other than work? Nothing. Why?"

"Because that text was from Ryan. He just confirmed with Jim that he's available to do the wedding. The Justice of the Peace is booked. I'm getting married!" She threw her arms around Jennifer and spun her in circles. Dizzy and breathless with excitement the two of them collapsed onto the nearest bench.

"What are you going to wear? What colour should I be wearing? Are you getting a long dress?"

"I'm going retro. I have an off-white suit with a matching hat that perches on the side of my head. My hair will be styled in a forty's-page and I have suede heels that also match. I plan on carrying a nosegay of baby's breath and red roses. I found a silver fox fur coat at a garage sale, I'll wear that as well when we go to the falls for our pictures."

Jennifer took it all in. Marcia, tall and slender, would be beautiful.

"What colour would you like me to wear? Should I wear a dress or suit?"

"Would you consider a suit? Something retro?"

"Of course."

"Let's run over to the consignment shop and see what they have. I asked the owner weeks ago to keep an eye open for me. She's been shopping around for a suit for you." Jennifer could barely keep up with Marcia as they hurried to the car. On the way over to the shop, Marcia babbled happily about the details for her wedding. She and Ryan were taking a three-day honeymoon to a resort up north.

"I'll be back Tuesday morning, I promise," she said as she pulled into a parking spot. "Have you been to this store yet?"

"No, I haven't. I'm curious though."

"You're going to love it. Sherri's the owner, she's an expert on retro fashion. Ryan got his suit here. Jim will be down Thursday, she had his measurements and found one for him too, a grey pinstripe. He'll wear a red tie. Ryan's tie will be white."

A bell above the door clanged as they entered.

"I started planning this wedding the day I met Ryan."

"I'm not surprised." Jennifer laughed and squeezed Marcia's arm. "He fell in love with you at first sight, it was obvious."

"Me too." Marcia sighed happily.

"Marcia!" Jennifer startled. The booming voice didn't match the genteel decor. Sherri was a large, boisterous woman who took up a lot of room with her broad frame and equally big personality. "You must be Jennifer. Nice to meet you!"

Jennifer tried not to wince as Sherri pumped her hand in a death grip.

"Now, let's see. Turn. Turn." She spun Jennifer around.

"Yes, I have it. I have the perfect suit." She turned to Marcia. "I brought in three to pick from but we don't need them. You described her perfectly, just perfectly. The first one will do nicely." She swept out of the room, returning almost immediately with a suit on her arm.

It was the colour of the Canadian flag, a bright cheerful red. Jennifer had envisioned having to wear a blouse, but this suit was its own outfit. She felt a tiny tingle of excitement at the thought of trying something so lovely on.

"Come, come, you must get fitted." Marcia smiled as Sherri grabbed Jennifer's wrist and dragged her to the back dressing room, closing the curtains with a swoosh.

"Shoes, I have the shoes too, Marcia." Sherri disappeared into her back room. Marcia poked her head around the curtain.

"Isn't Sherri awesome? I love her to bits."

"She likes to 'twin' words, doesn't she," said Jennifer in a low voice. "Turn, turn, come, come."

The two of them grinned at each other. Jennifer had not felt that fussed-over in a long time and it felt good.

"Size seven, like you asked for Marcia." Sherri's big hand almost dwarfed the red suede shoes that she handed Jennifer around the corner of the curtain.

"What's new, Sherri?" Marcia asked, giving Jennifer a chance to catch her breath and try on the suit and shoes. She heard Sherri and Marcia discussing an antique clutch that Sherri had recently acquired.

Turning her back to the mirror, Jennifer slipped into the suit, marvelling at the material and detail. The shoes were a perfect fit and as she looked down at her feet, she knew she was going to love the result. She turned to the mirror and caught her breath. She hardly knew the beautiful, stylish young woman in the mirror. She looked like she belonged to another era. She twirled in front of the mirror several times.

"Oh, Marcia. Look!" She pulled back the curtain. The look on Marcia and Sherri's face said it all. "If I look this good, you will be stunning."

"Marcia is stunning," Sherri said. "Her suit looks like it was made for her. It is couture, of course, the previous owner treasured it. Now, let's fit this hat." Sherri fussed and poked and pinned. Once again Jennifer turned to the mirror, bedazzled. She'd never felt so elegant and feminine.

"Have you and Ryan set a date yet?" asked Sherri.

"Friday," Marcia answered shyly.

"Good, very good," said Sherri. "No fuss, no muss, no major expenses, just you and Ryan and your attendants. Did you get in touch with the photographer I recommended?"

"Yes, Ryan did. He'll follow us around. We will go to the falls after the wedding. I hope we get a bit of sunshine."

"Then you must, you simply must show me the photos. I shall never forgive you if you don't. Never." She wagged her finger under Marcia's nose for emphasis.

"I will, I promise." Marcia smiled.

Jennifer had been looking around the store while Sherri and Marcia chattered. She was rather taken with it and made a mental note to come back. It was as cheerful and fun as it's owner. Sherri was starting to grow on her. She changed back to her funeral suit, and gave Sherri the shoes and suit.

"I'll pick everything up on Thursday," said Marcia as she handed Sherri her credit card.

"No Marcia, let me get this," Jennifer said.

"I wouldn't dream of it. I'm so happy to have you as my maid of honour."

After a boisterous goodbye from Sherri, the two friends walked back to the car.

"I should have paid for my own suit."

Marcia laughed. "It was forty dollars. The shoes were thirty and Sherri took care of the dry cleaning. You looked like a million dollars. She told me she found your suit crumpled in a box at a garage sale, the shoes buried at the bottom. It was the least I could do. I'm hungry. Want to get take out?"

"Sure. It's after five already. What a fun afternoon."

"It was, wasn't it? Sometimes I think we're so focused on work we forget to seek out lighter moments. Ryan is always reminding me to balance out my life more. Good advice."

They stopped to pick up a roasted chicken and salad and drove back to the funeral home. Jennifer's phone rang as they entered the garage door. It was Penny, Carol's sister. Jennifer was quickly yanked back into the present, Graham's murder had been trundling around the back of her mind throughout of the day.

"Hi, it's Penny. I won't keep you. It worked."

"It worked?" Jennifer didn't have a clue what Penny was alluding to.

"He corroborated her story. Carol's boyfriend. He owns a winery and is a big-wig in the area. Carol is being released tonight." Penny started to cry.

"I hope those are happy tears."

"Yes, they are. I can't thank you enough."

"I did nothing but listen. You found the tie, you approached the police and gave them the information."

"You supported me and gave me the courage to move forward. Thank you, Jennifer. Carol is going to try to see you tomorrow. She's exhausted and needs some alone time and rest right now."

"I'm so glad this ended on a happy note. When you're visiting your sister again, please set aside some time for me too."

"Oh, I will, for sure."

"Take care."

"What was that all about?" Marcia asked as they entered the apartment. The kitchen was gutted and it caught both of them off guard.

"Carol will be back to work tomorrow." She needed to change the subject, Marcia had a wedding on her mind and she didn't want to drag her into the mystery. "Wow. The workmen got a lot done today," she added as she walked over to the window and looked out. The dumpster at the edge of the building is almost full."

Marcia walked over to the porch. "The frame is in place for the screens. Your deck will be a great place to sit when it's done." Jennifer joined her and looked at the frame. "I should be able to enjoy it most of the year now. Grimsby can go outside too. I miss him."

"He misses you too, although Ryan may miss him more when he comes back home."

"Once the cupboards are installed I'll pick him up. You only have a few days before you get married."

"That reminds me, I made a hair appointment for us early Friday morning. We'll get our nails and make-up done too."

Jennifer looked down at her hand with her short, badly-shaped nails. "I don't have nails."

Marcia laughed. "You can have tips put on and a nice bright red polish to match your suit. If it bothers you, they can remove them the next day. I know you're thinking about work."

"I suppose I'm being silly. I'd love to have nice nails. It's the polish that bothers me. A funeral director with bright red nails shaking hands with a family member doesn't seem right somehow."

"A French manicure would work if you decide to have them done again," Marcia suggested kindly. "I used to get mine done all the time. I kind of got out of the habit when I moved down here."

"That's true, you always have been stylish." She started opening the food and went into the spare room to rummage through the boxes looking for plates and forks.

They sat on the sheet-covered furniture and discussed more about the wedding photos. The conversation turned to the renovation, and then to Carol's return.

"There's something I'm missing though," Jennifer mused forgetting she wasn't going to involve Marcia. She just couldn't shake the feeling she was overlooking something important.

"How so?"

"Graham's murder. If Carol didn't do it, who did?"

"Ryan said it was a tough case. The evidence pointed to Carol, as did the motive. He suspected something was amiss too. It didn't feel right."

Jennifer laughed. "Ryan doesn't usually base a case on feelings. He's a 'just the fact's ma'am' type of detective. Same as Anne's approach to journalism."

"I think we've helped him get in touch with his intuitive side," Marcia said. "Right from the start I didn't think Carol did it. He told me the evidence doesn't lie and I insisted it wasn't what it seemed."

"Me too. I have the feeling the answer is right under my nose." As she picked up her plate and went back toward the kitchen, Jennifer bumped a small table that held the plans and swatches that Agnes had neatly organized. Glancing down as she steadied the table, she paused.

The answer *was* right under her nose. It was on that little table, right out in the open.

'Marcia, look! I think we have proof that Carol didn't kill Graham." Marcia rushed over to see and a knowing smile inched across her lips.

Jennifer and Marcia talked late into the evening, discussing ways to prove Carol's innocence, and catch the killer.

11

Two calls over the next day kept Marcia and Jennifer busy. With four days until the wedding, Jennifer's excitement built exponentially. She was enjoying watching the plans unfold and happily distracted with wedding chatter.

Gordon Wilson, the new director, was due to start at William's on Tuesday. Marcia had finalized the details for a staff get-together and dinner at one of the restaurants overlooking the falls on Wednesday. Jim had called Jennifer about a gift for Marcia and Ryan, and the two of them agreed to go in on it together. Since Marcia and Ryan were deferring their island honeymoon for a later date, Jim had suggested he and Jennifer cover the cost. Jennifer readily agreed. Marcia was her dearest friend and Jim and Ryan were like brothers. They would give them the card at the wedding lunch, with the message that they could take the trip anytime it suited them.

Tuesday night Jennifer's friend Gwen stopped

by with chai lattes before she went to work. Her husband had been offered a promotion on the east coast—they were going to be moving in about six weeks.

"Is it going to be hard for you to give up your job at the casino?"

"I have mixed feelings," she said. "On one hand, I think it'll be good for the kids to experience a different region of the country. There is a casino in Halifax, maybe once we're settled I could consider applying. Or maybe I could start a bookkeeping service if I get bored. I don't have to work. We'll see."

"I'll miss you. I look forward to our late-night chats and chai lattes."

"Hard to believe I'll be in a different time zone and so far away. I never thought I'd ever leave this part of the country. But we can text back and forth and maybe you can visit sometime."

"It'll be a great opportunity for you and the kids and it gives me an excuse to visit." She gave Gwen a quick hug as she left. "If you need any help in the next six weeks, let me know."

Jennifer tossed the cups in the garbage and surveyed her kitchen. The wiring and plumbing were completed, the cupboards were to be installed tomorrow. The deck was almost done as well. She wondered if Carol would be back in the morning, she hadn't heard from her. Scanning the space one last time she turned off the lights and got ready for bed, mentally planning the busy few days ahead.

Agnes arrived at nine the next morning to meet the cabinet installers and take them upstairs. There was no sign of Carol. Jennifer watched the men unload the truck, wondering what to do next. She sought out Agnes.

"This is exciting. How long does it take them to do the installation?"

"They should be done by late afternoon. I don't anticipate any problems. I double-checked the measurements."

"We have an 11:00 a.m. service in the chapel and I have to run a few errands later today. Marcia's downstairs, have her text me if you need anything."

"Sure, I'll make sure there's no banging or hammering from 10:30 till noon. See you later."

"Thanks Agnes."

A few minutes before the service Jennifer was greeting people in the lobby when she saw Carol pull in.

"I'll be right back, Marcia. I don't want any of

the workmen to see Carol."

"You go, I've got this."

Slipping out the garage door, Jennifer stuck close to the building so she couldn't be seen from the second floor. Carol was getting out of her vehicle, dressed for work.

"Hey Carol, how are you? I'm so glad you were able to prove your alibi." She could hear movement on the deck above her head and she didn't want to be overheard. "Come, we have to talk."

Carol looked perplexed but followed Jennifer into the small hallway between the prep room and the garage. Carol spoke first.

"I'm so ashamed." Carol squeezed her eyes shut for a moment, likely battling with herself over her mistake. "I thought the police would know I was innocent. Now that the truth is out about my affair, Mark has been disgraced. His wife will divorce him, it'll affect his business and family."

"He made a choice. I can't believe you were willing to go to prison for him."

Carol looked at Jennifer, her eyes welling with tears. "I wasn't. He blamed me, like Graham blamed me for his problems. In the end, I knew I had to come clean to clear my name. I was hoping he loved me enough to come forward. I was wrong." Her shoulders slumped forward, defeat reflected in her voice. "You and Penny did what I should have done, told the truth from the beginning. The legal aid lawyer couldn't see me until the day of the hearing. Being in court and being charged was my wake-up call."

"Your sister wasn't going to quit until you were free. She knew you were innocent. So did I."

"Then who did it? I've spent all my time trying to figure that out. Do the police even have another suspect?"

"I don't know." She was being truthful. She hadn't mentioned her suspicions to Detective Constable Ziegler. At least, not yet. "You can't worry about who did it. That's up to the police now." That statement wasn't quite true, she was hoping to expose the killer later that day, that is, if the guilty party co-operated.

"My lawyer was helpful in more ways than one. She was young and kind and honest with me. She gave me the name of a counsellor and suggested I get support. The charges may have been dropped but I need to work on my self-esteem. I keep making excuses for people who walk all over me, like Graham. I went to university, have been successful in my own right, yet I seem to surround myself with people who use me. Maybe I let them."

"I'm glad you're back. We can talk later if you want. I have a service in a couple of minutes, then errands. Maybe I'll see you later in the day. Agnes is upstairs."

"I called her last night to tell her I'd be here."

The chapel service was a simple one with a small gathering of mourners. Jennifer would be taking the casket to the crematorium. She planned to stop at Williams to meet Gordon and pick up a few things before following through on her plan to expose the real killer. She spent the next hour giving her clients her full attention. The killer wasn't going anywhere.

The family left a few minutes before noon. Jennifer made sure they had no questions and had all the documentation.

As the door closed behind them, Marcia spoke up, "I'll run upstairs and let Carol and Agnes know they don't have to be quiet anymore."

"Thanks. I'm heading out as soon as we load the casket."

Marcia was back quickly and between the two of them the casket was loaded in a few minutes.

It was a cold day, the sun barely warming the

van as Jennifer drove to the crematorium. Her first stop on the way back was the pet store. She had Marcia devise a plan to trap the killer into confessing…and it involved a new bed for Grimsby.

"I hope this works," she muttered to herself as she put the bed in the back of the van. Her next stop was Williams Funeral Home to meet Gordon and welcome him. It was time to focus on her work and not on the murder. When she arrived, Jennifer found Desta in the front office.

"Hi, how's it going?

Desta looked up with a warm smile. "Good, Jennifer, you?"

"Same." She took off her coat and flipped it over a chair. "What do you think of Gordon?"

"He's quiet, the complete opposite of Brent."

Jennifer laughed. "Oh dear, wait until he sees Marcia and I together. I hope we don't scare him into quitting."

"No danger there, you and Marcia are a hoot together. And you're also two of the best funeral director's I know. I had no idea prior to taking this job that working in a funeral home could be so interesting. All of you have such a great sense of humour, not at all what I expected. We'll get him laughing in no time. He's downstairs with Brent, I think they're in the selection room."

"Thanks. See you on the way out."

Jennifer went downstairs, through the lounge to the selection room. The door was ajar and she pushed it open quietly and peeked around the corner. Brent and Gordon were deep in conversation. Brent saw her first.

"Jennifer, come in. This is Gordon." Gordon turned to greet her. He was tall and gangly, she guessed him to be her age or a bit younger. His blond hair was short, not a hair out of place. His funeral suit was tailored and his shoes spit-polished to perfection. Clearly, he was eager to make a good impression on his first day. She moved into the room and extended her hand.

"Welcome. I'm so happy to have you as part of the Spencer/William staff. His firm handshake and eye contact were reassuring. Brent had made a good choice. She got to the business at hand.

"Wednesday evening at 5:30, right after we lock up, I have organized a staff dinner so you can meet all of us. Is your girlfriend in Ottawa or did she come down with you?"

"She's in Ottawa. She's a nurse and works four shifts a week but she has applied to this area and has an interview on Friday at the hospital."

"I'm sorry she can't make it for the dinner. I hope she gets the job and can join you soon. Is Lori free, Brent?"

"She is, the sitter is organized. Looking forward to it."

"I still have to confirm Ryan, it depends on whether or not he has a call." She turned to Gordon. "Ryan is Marcia's fiancé, they'll be getting married this Friday. He is a Detective Sergeant with the Niagara Regional Police Homicide Division. Elaine, our office manager at Spencer's and her husband will be there, as will Desta and her husband, and Jeff. Unfortunately, Peter's at college, you'll meet him over Christmas. Needless to say, we are so pleased to have you with us. We've been a bit short-staffed and rather busy."

Gordon nodded. "The funeral home I worked in was small and quiet. We did a couple of calls a month. I worked on a farm with the understanding that if there was a death, I would leave immediately for the funeral home. I lived in Ottawa and the commute to the country every day was insane. I'm looking forward to being busy. I was excited when Brent hired me."

"If you worked on a farm, you're used to long hours, that's hard work. Now you have two funeral homes to work at. Brent can run you over to Spencer's for a tour when the two of you have time. Here's a key to the garage door." She passed him the key, which he transferred to his key chain.

"We will get to know each other soon, my day is getting away from me. See you later." She was anxious to get back to the funeral home.

On the drive back from Williams she rehearsed what she was going to say. It was nearly lunchtime and she was getting hungry. With her kitchen torn up, she'd skipped breakfast. Food was the first order of business, being hungry gave her brain-fog and she needed to be alert. Stopping at a drive-through she picked up a dozen muffins for her staff and Carol and the crew. Not the most nutritious, but it would tide her over.

When she pulled around to the back of the funeral home, she saw a furniture truck and felt a tiny rush of excitement. The office furniture had arrived, the last step in the downstairs renovations. Peter had given her some recommendations for laptops; she had purchased several and stored them away.

There were a few cars in the lot, some she recognized as Carol's and the workmen, but two were unfamiliar. Sure enough, Elaine was in the lounge and Marcia in the main office with a family.

"Oops," she said quietly to Elaine. "Has the family gone into the selection room yet?"

Elaine shook her head. "I'm keeping an eye out, although the furniture is nearly installed. The two installers have been quiet, I told them we had a family and they've been respectful. They said they could scoot out for lunch if Marcia took the family through. Mind you, the soundproofing is working, I haven't heard a thing from them."

Jennifer poked her head into the selection room. There was no evidence there were workmen in the area.

"They've taken the cardboard out to the dumpster and are installing one desk at a time. I think they're doing the last one now."

Jennifer took the time to have a cup of tea and a muffin, and put the rest of the muffins on the counter. Taking Grimsby's hammock upstairs she poked her head through the door. The apartment was a beehive of activity as two workmen, under the supervision of Carol, were completing the installation of the upper cabinets.

Carol greeted Jennifer with a cheerful, "Hi."

"Starting to take shape. It looks good," Jennifer said. "If any of you want a muffin, they're on the counter in the lounge. Is Agnes coming back today?"

"She should be here shortly. Did you need her for something?"

"Yep, nothing major. Would you let her know I'm looking for her?"

"Absolutely." As Carol turned back to her task, Jennifer put Grimsby's new bed in the closet and went back downstairs to her new office. Several more muffins and another cup of tea later she felt brighter and more alert. Marcia poked her head into the office and sat down.

"This office space is amazing. It's quietly tucked away. The new desks look great."

"At some point, maybe this afternoon, I have to unpack the laptops and initialize them."

"I can help. I popped in to tell you about the new family."

A gentle tap at the door interrupted them. Jennifer rose, opened it and found Agnes standing there.

"Hi!"

"You wanted to see me?"

"I was wondering if I could ask a favour."

"Sure." Agnes seemed a bit subdued, thought Jennifer. Having Carol back definitely put a damper on her taking charge of the rest of the renovations. *If it were me, I'd feel bad too.*

"You have a skill none of the rest of us has. Can you come upstairs, I'd appreciate your help. It shouldn't take too long. I'll be back in a few minutes Marcia."

"No problem. I could use a muffin and a cup of tea."

Wordlessly, Agnes followed Jennifer up to the apartment. There was no sign of Carol or the workmen. They were probably on lunch. Jennifer pulled the hammock from the bag.

"I got a new bed for Grimsby and I was wondering if you could tie that amazing knot you do. I want to put it on the deck so he can snooze when we're sitting outside. I bought some hooks, I can hang it later."

The colour seemed to drain from Agnes' face but she rallied quickly. Without a word, she took the hammock and within the space of a few minutes had tied both ends. Jennifer wanted to ask what kind of knot it was, but decided not to push her luck. She didn't want Agnes to become suspicious.

"Thank you, it's perfect."

"No problem." Agnes turned and abruptly left the apartment.

Exhaling slowly Jennifer took the hammock to

the bedroom, laid it on her bed and took a photo of the knots. She hid the hammock under some towels in the linen closet and went back downstairs.

Closing the door to the office, she sank into her chair with a sigh of relief.

"I got it." She pulled her phone and showed Marcia, who was chewing on her muffin.

"Good. Now we have to confront her."

"She left rather quickly. We'll have to wait for an opportune moment."

"Then back to the call. I can run over to the hospital in a few minutes. Kind of a sad call."

Jennifer cocked her head, listening intently to her friend.

"It's an elderly man and woman, Mr. & Mrs. Holden, who both died over the past twenty-four hours. They'd been married almost sixty-one years when she fell, was hospitalized and put on a waiting list for a nursing home. She was transferred there yesterday. He'd been able to visit her at the hospital, but the nursing home was too far away. She died about two hours after the move and was sent to the hospital for an autopsy.

"According to the daughter, all she talked about was her husband when they were separated. She kept asking them to take her home. When the family informed their dad that mom had passed away, apparently he didn't say a word. He went to bed last night and one of the grandsons, who was staying with him, found him in the morning. He died in his sleep." She took a sip of her tea. "The family was going to call us this morning to arrange their mom's funeral, now they have two. I told them we would put them together in the suite. I ordered an extra funeral coach for the funeral on Thursday."

Jennifer shook her head. "That is sad. Has the dad been released?"

"Their doctor came to the house and signed the death certificate. You were out, so I sent Jeff and Gordon to pick him up. He's in the prep room. Mrs. Holden was just released."

"I'll go with you to the hospital then, we can work together. The last thing you need is to lift someone and have a set-back before the wedding."

"The family will be back with the clothing in a while. They chose the same casket for both of them, one with a peach interior for their mother and the other with a pale blue interior for their dad. It was a challenge for them losing both their parents so fast. We had the peach interior casket in the selection room, Jeff will get the one with the blue interior out of the storage area at Williams and drop it off later today."

"Brent was going to try to drop by with Gordon and orient him at some point today. Maybe he could help with prep. He worked at a funeral home that did about twenty-five calls a year. He could be a bit rusty. It'll give us a chance to assess his skill level. He can help you with one, I'll give you a hand with the second one."

Marcia looked at her thoughtfully. "Should be fun, I haven't had to 'break anyone in' since you were under my supervision in Toronto." She gave Jennifer a fiendish look and they both laughed.

"Why am I laughing," said Jennifer. "I was terrified of you. For that matter, so was Jeff and he was support staff."

"Operative word—*was*. I have high standards but I'm fair."

"I often wonder whether or not I'd still be in funeral service if it wasn't for you. I came awfully close to quitting that first year."

"You didn't have much confidence," said Marcia kindly. "But you had more heart than anyone I've ever seen. You worked hard and tried harder. Look at you now."

Jennifer smiled wanly. "I don't always feel competent."

"Neither do I. But we do make a fearsome team."

"Don't we, though."

They were interrupted by the front door; the Holden family had arrived with clothing. Marcia introduced Jennifer and they spent a few minutes reviewing details with them. After the family left, Marcia let Elaine know they were off to do a transfer and asked her to call Gordon to see if he wanted to join her in the prep room in about an hour if he was free.

"When do you think you're going to confront Agnes?" Marcia asked as they drove to the hospital.

"Sooner rather than later. I find myself getting cold feet. When I watched her tie those knots on Grimsby's hammock today I knew she had something to do with Graham's murder. I didn't want to believe it. She must have had help."

"You'll be fine, she likes you and maybe she'll tell you the truth. We have to let Detective Constable Ziegler know soon too."

"You're right. I think I should tell her now, rather than later. I don't want it to look like I was meddling. Speaking of Grimsby, do you think I could pick him up after work?"

"Hmm, Ryan might have something to say

about that. He loves that cat. But I think Grimsby misses you, so follow me home and we can have dinner."

"Great, thanks. I've missed him too."

Jennifer called the main police line and left a message for Sue, telling her she had some important information about Graham's murder and to call her as soon as she was free.

The transfer was quick and smooth. Back at the funeral home, Gordon was waiting for them. He'd brought the casket with the blue lining from Williams.

"Hi Gordon, this is Marcia." Gordon shook Marcia's hand then helped her transfer Mrs. Holden to the prep room.

"That's sad," he said as he looked at the elderly couple.

"I'm not so sure," Marcia said thoughtfully. "It's hard for the family, but they were together for so many years. I'm inclined to think it must have been too hard on Mr. Holden to be without his wife."

"It's true. You often do see people who have been married for a long time die within a few days of each other. If it were me, I wouldn't want to be alone either," he admitted.

"I heard you have a fiancé. Tell me about her."

Jennifer excused herself and left the two of them to get started. She was eager to go upstairs and see if Agnes was there.

Carol and the workmen were putting the finishing touches on the lower cabinets. The counter had been installed. Jennifer stood and looked at her new kitchen, her mouth hanging open.

"What do you think?"

"Wow Carol. I am at a loss for words."

"The island goes in tomorrow, your appliances will be here tomorrow morning, a few touch ups and you'll have your life back. We should be out of here by noon."

"Are you expecting Agnes anytime soon?"

Carol looked at her solemnly. "Let's go downstairs, I could use a coffee." She turned to the workmen. "Do you guys want a coffee?"

"Naw, we're nearly done. Thanks though."

Jennifer's intuition told her something was wrong. It didn't take Carol long to get to the point once they'd made their beverages and sat down.

"Agnes quit."

Jennifer's heartrate accelerated. She did her best to keep her voice calm and level, "Did she say why?"

"She blames me for Graham's death. She told

206

me in no uncertain terms that she thinks I'm guilty. She demanded I mail her final pay to her mother's house and said she hoped to never see me again." Carol's voice was quiet and subdued as she looked up at Jennifer.

"I wasn't expecting that. Agnes was a solid employee. I've been such a fool." Tears spilled from her eyes and tracked down her cheeks.

"Penny told me how Graham had taken your money and used it for drugs and partying."

"It's not that, it's the fact that I tried to cover up my latest relationship. But yes, I also kept hoping Graham would turn things around."

"I don't mean to be nosy, but are you going to be able to continue the business?"

"I hope so. There's a little apartment on top of the shop. I can sell my house. It might be enough to keep the store open. I have to try, it's all I've got."

"You're a talented designer, I love the work you've done for me. Williams will need a few renovations, you can count on my business."

"Thanks." She stood up and walked to the sink to rinse her cup. "I grew to hate Graham. Hate is such a destructive emotion. I often wondered how Agnes felt about him. She never talked about herself or her feelings." She turned off the tap and dried her hands. "I hope she's going to be OK."

"You need to think about yourself right now," said Jennifer kindly. "Agnes is an adult, she can take care of herself. She chose to quit."

"Yeah, I have a lot to think about and some major changes to make. I wish Agnes had talked me to about how she felt." She sighed. "I'd better get up there.

"You got it done a lot faster than I thought it would be."

"Timeline's can be escalated."

"See you tomorrow then."

Jennifer went into her office and closed the door. Once at her desk she put her head in her hands. What was she going to now? If she told the police she'd planned to confront Agnes, Sue and Ryan would not be impressed. If she didn't tell them about the knot, Agnes could go free. There was no question she had to come clean. She'd already left that voicemail for Sue.

12

It was after six that evening before Detective Constable Ziegler returned Jennifer's call. Gordon and Marcia were finishing up in the prep room, Gordon had offered to stay and help with both embalmings. Elaine had gone home, locking the doors behind her. Jennifer used the time to distract herself with paperwork and bills, trying not to think about Sue's call.

"Hi Jennifer, I got your message. What's up?"

"There's something you should know about Graham's murder."

"Oh?" Sue was all business, her tone made that clear. Jennifer's heart sank. Taking a deep breath, she plunged into the matter at hand.

"There was something about Graham's murder that bothered me. It came to me yesterday. There was a knot tied in the measuring tape around his neck. I know who tied it, at least I'm almost sure I do. Only one person I know could have done it."

"Go on."

"I thought if I got the person to tie the knot again, then confront them, you'd know for sure. But I think she was on to us."

"Us? What do you mean by that?"

"Well, uh, me. I discussed it with Marcia. The plan was to confront her today but she quit."

"Jennifer, you're not making much sense. I'll get back to you in a few minutes, OK?"

"OK."

Sue hung up without another word.

Jennifer sat back in her chair, eyes closed. She was nauseous with fear. In hindsight, she hadn't used the best judgment trying to trap Agnes and there could be consequences. It didn't take long before her phone rang again. It was Detective Sergeant Gillespie and he wasn't happy.

"I want you and Marcia down here immediately. You do not compare notes, you do not talk to each other. Is that clear?"

Jennifer could barely swallow let alone respond.

"Is that clear?" he repeated.

"Yes," she replied meekly. "Marcia is in the prep room. I'll let her know."

"Never mind, I'll let her know. You get in your car and come now." He hung up.

Shaking, she didn't even bother to take the time

211

to change her suit. She picked up her keys and left. She blamed herself. Agnes could get away with murder. She would do her best not to involve Marcia. If Ryan was angry with Marcia two days before the wedding, Jennifer would never forgive herself if they broke it off.

How could I have been so stupid?

She was hungry and tired, she'd barely eaten all day and was not at her best. But the thought of stopping to eat added to the queasiness her anxiety triggered. She hoped it wouldn't take too long.

At the police station, she approached the front desk.

"Jennifer Spencer to see Detective Sergeant Gillespie."

"Hang on." The officer picked up the phone. "Ms. Spencer is here." He hung up and looked at her. "He'll be right out."

She turned to take a seat in the waiting room but barely took a few steps before Ryan opened the door. Neither spoke as she followed him to the back. He led her to the conference room where Sue was waiting, and closed the door. She looked around the familiar room and took a seat as far away from the two of them as possible. There were no cheery greetings this time.

"Is your phone off?"

She nodded and checked to see if her pager was on vibrate.

"Start from the top." Ryan sat back in his chair, arms folded. Sue tapped her pen on the table, head down.

"I told you that when I found Graham, I noticed Carol's measuring tape around his neck." Both detectives looked at her wordlessly. She soldiered on. "Something wasn't right, I couldn't get a handle on it until the other night."

Silence. If only the ground would open up and swallow her, or her pager go off.

"It was the knot in the measuring tape. I'd seen it several times before. Agnes tied *her* measuring tape that way. I'm sure you saw that in the crime scene photos."

Again, no answer. She was starting to prickle with sweat.

"So, I thought if I could get Agnes to incriminate herself by tying a knot for me, then I could confront her. Unfortunately..." Sue stopped tapping the pen. "Agnes quit."

The air was pregnant with silence, it hung over them like a thundercloud.

"I took a photo," she said lamely.

Ryan's feet hit the floor with a bang as he uncrossed his arms and slammed forward. "What the hell were you two thinking, Jennifer?"

"I'm sorry. I did call Sue to tell her." Tears threatened to surface.

"You interfered with a homicide investigation. You had no right to confront Agnes, let alone entrap her." He shook his head as if to shake off his disgust.

"Do you have a picture of the knot?" Sue asked.

She nodded and pulled her phone out. She lowered it beneath the level of the table because she was shaking and flipped to the photo of Grimsby's hammock. Wordlessly Sue looked at it and passed it to Ryan.

"Send it to me," he said. The phone rang near Sue and she picked it up.

"Ziegler. Thank you." Sue nodded at Ryan who, without another word, left the conference room.

"Do you have any idea where Agnes might be now?" Sue asked as Jennifer took her phone out of meeting mode to send the photo to Ryan.

"No."

"What made you think she was suspicious when you asked her to tie the knot?"

"The look on her face."

"What look?"

214

The questions were relentless and went on and on. Ryan did not return. Jennifer was hoping it would be over soon. Her stomach growled, her head ached, and her hunger made her a bit shaky, but Sue started again with the same line of questioning. Finally, she stopped and made a statement, "I think you realize your mistake. This isn't the movies. You were not to talk to anyone about this case and you involved your colleague, Ryan's fiancé. They're supposed to get married Friday and right now, Ryan is *not* thinking about a wedding, he's thinking about what the two of you did. Agnes could be long gone. We need evidence, not wild speculation over a knot. It is not your job to get that evidence."

At the mention of the wedding, Jennifer's resolve crumbled and she broke. Sue sat immobile while she sobbed. When she had composed herself, Sue spoke again.

"If you speak to anyone about this again, you could be charged with interfering in an investigation. Do you understand?"

Not trusting herself to speak. Jennifer nodded.

"Did you touch the knot?"

"No."

"Then I'll send an officer back with you to take it as evidence. You may wait in the front lobby." Sue rose, opened the door and escorted Jennifer out in silence. There was no sign of Marcia or Ryan. Ten minutes later, just before 9:00 p.m. an officer followed her back to her apartment. As Jennifer drove, her stomach alternated between hunger and nausea, anxious to get rid of the officer and be alone.

When they arrived at the funeral home he waited just inside the door as she went up to her apartment. Wordlessly she handed him a bag with Grimsby's hammock. She locked the door behind him and went to the lounge to make tea, spilling it as she walked up the stairs. She was trembling again. She rummaged around for cookies and finished off the bag, all the while willing Marcia to call or text, but there was only her and her anxiety—and silence. It was a long, lonely, sleepless night as she alternated between anxiety for Marcia and her sense of failure in trying to catch a murderer.

Early the next morning, unable to sleep or quiet her mind, Jennifer got ready for her day. She got in her car, stopped at a drive through, and put her breakfast on the seat beside her she drove to the falls. The wind was cold, the Christmas decorations blowing in the icy blast. She found a bench and sat and ate, barely tasting her food.

Restless, she tossed the bag in the garbage, sat and sipped her coffee and looked up and down the walkway. Usually, she enjoyed the cold, this time it seemed to pass right through her. Shivering, she decided to go back to the warmth of the funeral home. They had a double funeral to prepare for. She was plagued with guilt and a sense of failure, and was afraid to face her best friend.

Pulling up to her spot near the garage she noticed Bloom's Flower van parked at the garage door. Scrambling to let John in to do his delivery, she was surprised to find the door open. It was only 8:00 a.m. but John was chatting with Marcia, who shot her a quick *I have to talk to you* look.

"Hi John, how's it going?" Jennifer faked her cheerfulness.

"Good, Jennifer. Kinda sad, a double funeral."

"It is." That statement to John she didn't have to fake.

"I'll catch you two later." As the door closed behind him, Marcia grabbed her by the sleeve and pulled her into the lounge, pushing her into a chair. Marcia sat down across from her.

"I'm sorry Marcia. I'm so sorry." She could feel tears stinging her eyes, and she fought them.

"Boy, was Ryan pissed."

"We aren't allowed to discuss it."

"True. However, I did not kill that designer and Ryan got an earful from me about his attitude. I'm his fiancé, not his suspect."

Jennifer was speechless. She opened her mouth to respond, then shut it again.

"I get that we interfered. I apologized. To hear him yelling and carrying on you'd think we were criminals."

It was too much for Jennifer. She started to cry and this time she didn't hold back.

"Oh don't, please don't. I didn't mean to upset you." She stood up. "Coffee?"

Jennifer nodded as she collected herself and watched Marcia make the coffee. "Sue told me that with your wedding tomorrow, Ryan wasn't thinking about it, he was thinking about what we did. I should never have brought you into this. I wasn't supposed to talk to anyone about it and I did, I talked to Penny, Carol's sister and you. I feel terrible."

"Ryan started asking question after question. I admitted that I had talked to you, and should have stayed out of it, but he was like a dog with a bone." She set Jennifer's coffee down, then sat across from her.

"How long were you at the station?"

"Five minutes. He had his coat on when he met me in the lobby. I followed him in my car. We were barely in the door to my apartment before he exploded." She giggled. "At first I was upset, I didn't want to cause problems for the investigation, then I decided to let him run out of steam. I stayed calm, kept answering his constant barrage of questions while I made dinner, set the table, and when I put the dinner in front of him, he barely noticed." She took a sip of her coffee.

"When he brought up how he was disappointed in me, I started to cry. Seriously, he knows I'm not stupid. I did feel bad. Ryan had never seen me cry. He did a one-eighty. I sincerely hope I don't become the kind of wife who uses tears to get her way, he turned to putty."

"The wedding is still on?" Jennifer could barely speak the words.

"Of course. In fact, after the funeral today, I'm going to take off early, pick up the suits, check with the lunch venue, and pay a few bills."

"I'll pick up Grimsby after work, sorry I couldn't get him last night."

"Oh no! Grimsby! He's in the garage." She slammed her cup onto the table and flew out of the room. Jennifer smiled, calmly put her cup down and

219

met Marcia in the garage. She'd picked up Grimsby in his carrier and was apologizing profusely to him.

"Hi buddy," said Jennifer softly. He greeted her with a chirp.

"I can't believe I forgot about him," Marcia groaned.

"He's fine, it's not the first time he's had to wait in his carrier. I'll take him upstairs. Thanks for bringing him."

"I'm so sorry Grimsby," continued Marcia. "I didn't mean to forget about you. Give him some treats from me," she yelled to Jennifer as she disappeared into her apartment.

After depositing Grimsby in her bedroom with fresh food and water and his litter, she came back down to find Marcia starting to set up for the funeral. Together they completed the set-up and waited for the family, focussing on the details of the job, their earlier conversation forgotten.

After an hour's visitation with friends, the celebrant met with the family as Jennifer and Marcia set up the chapel. The lounge was busy with visitors. Elaine kept an eye on the coffee. Ten minutes before the service, Jennifer saw the two funeral coaches pull up by the chapel doors. She watched with a tiny smile as Jeff directed Gordon where to park. A staff member from the limo service parked behind the coaches with the family car.

Marcia asked Gordon to assist with the service. After the family was seated they wheeled in Mrs. Holden first, then Mr. Holden.

Jennifer led Jeff to the lounge. "How are you and Gordon getting along?"

"He's a great guy. He was a little unsure of himself initially, but that's to be expected, he's used to working in a rural area. I didn't have a clue when I first started. You know, Marcia should become the official trainer for both funeral homes, she's really good at it."

Jennifer looked at Jeff thoughtfully. He had a point, Marcia was a good trainer and she enjoyed it. She made a mental note to ask Marcia if she wanted to take on that role. She had a feeling Marcia would jump at the chance.

Jennifer watched as the service ended. Jeff went out to the coaches and opened the back doors. Marcia and Gordon wheeled out Mrs. Holden first and Marcia directed the pallbearers. When she and Gordon wheeled out Mr. Holden, she let Gordon direct the pallbearers. *Marcia's a natural teacher. I'm sure Brent would be happy to have her take over that role as well. I'll ask her next week.*

Jennifer stayed at the funeral home to tidy up. The afternoon was almost over and tomorrow was Marcia's wedding day. Jennifer could hardly wait to see Jim again. It would be a grand day. She'd put yesterday's incident at the police station out of her mind. It was time to move on. Shortly after she said goodnight to Elaine and locked up for the evening, her phone rang. It was Detective Constable Ziegler. Sue sounded a little warmer and friendlier as she asked Jennifer a few more questions about Agnes. One of her questions was if she had seen Agnes talking with anyone at the funeral home. Jennifer hesitated before she told Sue that she had seen Agnes with the same workman they had questioned earlier. "I think his name was Antonio."

"Why didn't you bring this up the other night?"

"Two reasons. First, the meeting, if can call it that, took place in the funeral home—Agnes didn't talk much. Antonio was the only one I saw her have a conversation with. Second reason? Because I was tired and hungry and the two of you grilled me like a suspect. I'm surprised I was able to give you the information I did." Jennifer closed her eyes realizing how accusatory it sounded. Sue had done everything she could to help her previously when she'd been under police protection and she respected her for it.

She also remembered how upset Sue was when she was pulled from the protection detail.

There was a pause before Sue responded.

"I'm sorry Jennifer. We were a little hard on you. The only thing you were guilty of was interfering in an investigation. At this point, it isn't a crime and I know you won't cross that line again. We all make mistakes."

"I feel bad that I might have scared Agnes off."

"We'll find her eventually. I'll let you go, you have a wedding to go to tomorrow. Goodnight Jennifer."

"Goodnight Sue."

The relief she felt was instant. It was kind of her to call. Sue knew how sensitive Jennifer could be and how she took things to heart. She smiled to herself as she thought of Marcia standing up to Ryan.

Taking one last trip around the funeral home to make sure everything was ready for the next day, she went upstairs. Opening the door to her apartment she stopped in surprise. The LED lighting gave the apartment a different atmosphere. The kitchen was beautiful. A bowl of fruit with a card propped up against it sat on the island. The new appliances gleamed. Grimsby rubbed up against her, meowing.

223

Carol must have let him out of the bedroom as she was leaving.

"You're trying to tell me this isn't the same as it was a week ago, Grimsby?" She plucked him off the floor and he settled in her arms, purring contentedly. She walked around the island with him and inspected the kitchen from all angles. The deck was lit softly and it looked inviting with the new all-weather furniture. The only thing missing was Grimsby's hammock. A tiny twinge of guilt zapped her as she thought about the knots.

"I think I'll order take-out tonight," she said to her cat. "I can get groceries later. While we are waiting for that, I'm going to put everything back in the kitchen." She called in an order for Chinese food, changed into her jeans and got to work. She explored the empty cupboards, making decisions where things should go. There was a lot more room in her new kitchen and she was thrilled.

"First order of business is the coffee pot," she said to Grimsby, who had moved to his favourite spot on the couch and was watching her with interest. She dragged the boxes out of the spare room and started unpacking. Once the coffee maker was tucked into the corner of the counter, she stood back and admired it. It didn't take long to put everything away.

Carol had suggested a built-in pantry and Jennifer was delighted when all the cans and dry goods fit with plenty of room left over. The delivery person called from the garage door downstairs and, after retrieving the food she sat at the island in her kitchen, staring out the window into the night. It was fun to wash her dishes in her new double sink and she took her time, wiping down the counters and rearranging the spices. A call from Anne interrupted her puttering.

"Can you pick me up at the airport tomorrow?"

"Toronto?

"Yep."

No. I can't, it's Marcia's wedding day. What time are you arriving?"

"Around four. Shoot."

"You still have your key for the funeral home, right?"

"Yeah."

"Well, book the airport shuttle and let yourself in. I don't know what time I'll be home. Hopefully I won't be too late. Even if I am, you can make yourself comfortable. There will be some leftover Chinese food in the fridge."

"Looks like I don't have a choice. I'll rent a car

at the airport instead," grumbled Anne.

"How long are you staying?"

"Till Tuesday morning. I told you I would be coming."

"You told me you would be coming, yes, but you didn't say when. It's been a few weeks since we talked."

"I wanted to stay at the cottage."

"Then Saturday morning, if I don't have a call, we can open it up and get you some groceries. It won't kill you to spend one night here."

"Fine. See you tomorrow." Anne hung up without another word.

Jennifer smiled. She was looking forward to seeing her cantankerous other half. Chances were Anne would be happy in the spare room. Clearly her sister was tired and stressed. Once they had time to talk and rest, they'd go out. Anne would wind down and be a little easier to get along with. *Funny how we are so different*. She suspected Anne had few friends in Ottawa. She was obsessed with work and didn't take the time to develop and nurture friendships.

After watching TV and catching up on the news on her laptop, Jennifer ran a bubble bath and soaked for a while. She and Marcia were meeting at 8:00

a.m. at the hairdressers. Gordon was covering the funeral home and Brent was available if he needed help. Marco would be doing both hairdos, and their makeup and manicures would be done while the other one was getting their hair done. Marco had promised to get them both out by 10:30. He was going to pin their hats on for them, since they'd be at the falls and the wind could be gusty. They'd go back to Marcia's apartment, change into their suits and be ready by 11:00 a.m. Marcia wasn't superstitious, she didn't care if they saw each other before the wedding, neither did Ryan.

After her bath, she made herself a cup of tea and curled up with a book. Grimsby nudged her around 11:00 p.m. "Off you go buddy, I'm on the last chapter. I'll be in shortly." Grimsby disappeared into the bedroom. *I think he missed his routine.* She turned back to her novel. A short while later she climbed into bed, contented and happy. Her best friend was getting married. Life didn't get any better.

13

Waking to a winter sun the next morning, Jennifer checked the time—a few minutes before 7:00 a.m. She wandered out to her kitchen and made herself a coffee, savouring the freedom of a day away from her job. She had a quick shower and washed her hair, it would save time later. She made sure Grimsby had what he needed and then picked up her suit on its hanger, the hatbox and her overnight bag. She drove to the mall, arriving a few minutes before eight. Marcia was already there, getting a shampoo.

The manicurist took Jennifer to the back and pulled the red hat from the box, setting it on the counter. Jennifer looked at it in wonder, she could hardly believe she was wearing something so unique and pretty. After trying dozens of colours, the manicurist recommended a bright red.

"You don't think it's too much?" Jennifer was fascinated by the bright colour sample sitting on her fingernail.

"Not at all." The manicurist smiled. "Round or square?" Jennifer looked at her, feeling dumb. "What do you recommend?"

"How about a sports length round. It shouldn't interfere with your work. When was your last manicure?"

"This is my first," Jennifer said sheepishly. She had to admit she was a bit nervous about having her nails done, let alone having them tipped and coloured.

"You are going to love it. Relax and enjoy."

Jennifer did enjoy watching the process, she was fascinated. She wasn't sure she was quite at the stage of accepting it as the manicurist adeptly snipped, filed, glued and shaped her right hand, then started on the left one. Less than an hour later, she was staring at both hands in fascination. She couldn't believe the transformation. Her hands look like they belong to someone else, not her. Those were the hands of an elegant, sophisticated woman.

"Ready Melissa," the manicurist yelled before giving Jennifer last minute instructions about what *not* to do with her new nails.

Melissa led Jennifer to another chair and began her makeup, turning her away from the mirror. Jennifer wanted to look as natural as possible and

Melissa agreed to comply. Twenty minutes later as Melissa swung the chair back to the mirror, Jennifer gasped with pleasure. She barely recognized herself.

"Ready!" Marco led Marcia around the corner. The staff stopped to look. Marcia was glowing. Marco assisted her into the makeup chair, grinning with delight at his work.

"Wow," Marcia and Jennifer spoke simultaneously as they saw each other.

"Chop, chop," Marco said, interrupting their moment of mutual admiration. He ushered Jennifer to his chair on the other side of the wall before she could say another word. Sitting in place, she pulled her left hand out from under the cape and placed it in her lap, staring in fascination at the strange appendage with the red tips. Marco tucked cotton strips around her face to protect her makeup as he wet down her hair with a spray bottle and picked up his scissors.

A few minutes before 10:30 the two of them walked out of the salon, Jennifer feeling as if she was someone else. She barely recognized the elegant woman she'd become.

On the way back to Marcia's apartment Jennifer texted Ryan with Marcia's phone to let him know they were on their way. He texted back to say the flowers had been delivered and he and Jim were almost ready.

"How are you feeling?" Jennifer asked Marcia.

"I hardly know. My emotions are all over the place." She glanced over at Jennifer and smiled. "I'm excited, happy, honoured, my stomach has a zillion butterflies. Maybe I'm a tiny bit nervous, it's hard to say. I simply can't believe that Ryan is waiting for me, that I will be his wife." She started to choke up.

"Don't cry! You'll ruin your makeup." The two of them laughed. Jennifer was close to tears herself she was so happy for her friend. "Did you call your mother?"

Marcia sighed. She and her mother were not close; she barely spoke about her. Her mother was a single parent who'd remarried when Marcia was six. Being the oldest, she practically raised her stepbrother and sister. Her mother moved to Spain with the younger siblings when Marcia was 18, a year after Marcia left home for college.

"I called her. She said to send a picture. Not *congratulations* or *I'm happy for you.*"

"I'm sorry. We both keep hoping our mom's will at least attempt to be mothers once in a while. It doesn't happen, but we keep trying."

"Ryan and Jim will be over in about ten minutes," Marcia said, as she unlocked the door to her condo. "Jim spent the night at Ryan's place. They probably talked until morning." It only took a couple of minutes for the two of them to change into their suits, Jennifer in one room, Marcia in another.

"Ready?" asked Jennifer.

"Ready!

"On the count of three—one, two, three." Like teenagers getting ready for prom, they stepped out into the living room and faced each other.

"Oh, Marcia. Oh! You are the most beautiful bride I have ever seen."

Marcia looked as if she had stepped off a 1930's Vogue magazine cover. Her dark hair glistened with shiny waves. The winter white hat with its tiny veil added to the dramatic effect. The suit, with the high collar, elegant lines and a straight skirt that ended mid-calf, suited her 5 foot 7-inch slim figure. She was a vision of beauty and elegance. Her suede shoes, a perfect match, completed the outfit.

"I do dress up nicely, don't I," said Marcia.

"I'll say. You're stunning!"

"You look pretty good yourself. Red is such a flattering colour for you."

"I don't usually wear red. I kind of like it."

A tap on the door meant Jim was letting them know it was time to go. Jennifer opened the door to see her former protection officer and Ryan's friend.

"Jim!" He stepped into the apartment and swept her up in a hug. "You look incredible. You've lost weight. Are you not taking care of yourself?" His retro suit was perfect for his build. He could have been a gangster or a banker from that era. His tie matched her suit perfectly.

"Maybe a little," he said shyly. "I've been working out a bit."

He looked over at Marcia, who stood quietly in the middle of the room.

"Is this beautiful creature the soon to be Mrs. Gillespie? You look like a goddess Marcia."

"Thank you, Jim."

"Ryan. Your bride awaits." Jim moved aside as Ryan entered the room. Jennifer watched as his gaze connected with Marcia's and his face transformed. His eyes glinted with tears. Marcia still had not moved, as she looked at Ryan—her face said it all.

"Let's get Marcia's flowers, shall we?" Jim was keeping everyone on time. Jennifer went with Jim to Ryan's apartment, picked up the flowers and crossed the hall.

"I've got your purse and flowers, Marcia. Your

coat and gloves are on the back of the chair. We'll see you downstairs in a few minutes."

Marcia broke Ryan's gaze long enough to focus on what was said. She looked at Jennifer and nodded. "Thanks."

As the door closed, Marcia moved toward Ryan. Jennifer hadn't even noticed his suit, she'd been so caught up in his reaction to seeing his bride.

Jennifer stood in the lobby as Jim pulled the car up. They were using a white Lincoln lead car from the limo service both funeral homes used. It gleamed in the winter sun. Jim opened the front door to the passenger side and Jennifer settled in.

Less than five minutes later, Ryan and Marcia emerged, arm in arm. Marcia handed the fur coat to Jim, who placed it in the back seat. The photographer materialized from nowhere to capture the moment. Jim opened the door for Marcia as Ryan walked around to the other side. The drive to City Hall was short, no one spoke.

Jennifer turned to hand Marcia her flowers and accepted Jim's hand as she emerged from the car. Jim then opened the door for Marcia and watched as Ryan came around and took her gloved hand, helping her out. He tucked her hand under his arm and waited until Jim took Jennifer's arm. Together the four of them entered City Hall and went to the Office of the Justice of the Peace.

It was a busy Friday morning and people stopped to watch as Marcia and Ryan, followed by Jennifer and Jim, walked past them. Exclamations of surprise greeted them.

"Oh, look!"

"How beautiful."

The Justice rose as they entered the office. He was a tiny little bald man with an endearing grin. He reached out and shook Ryan's hand.

"Good morning Detective. This must be your beautiful bride, and beautiful she is." Jim handed him the marriage licence, and the Justice scanned it.

"Yes. Yes. Well. Shall we begin?"

Marcia handed Jennifer her flowers and gloves and turned to face Ryan, taking both his hands. The ceremony was simple and as Jennifer heard the time-honoured words, 'til death do you part', the thought crossed her mind that funerals and weddings were similar in their solemnity. Marcia seemed to be floating on a cloud of serenity, her calm demeanour and beauty adding a layer of dignity to the drab little office.

With the pronouncement, "I now declare you to be husband and wife, you may kiss your bride," it was over. The four of them signed the marriage licence and thanked the JP. Marcia put on her gloves and took her flowers from Jennifer.

As they left the office a thunder of applause greeted Marcia and Ryan. Dozens of police officers and office staff stood along the hall and applauded as a surprised Ryan and Marcia laughed and accepted the congratulations of Ryan's peers. As Jennifer walked past Sue and Haney, Sue caught her eye, nodded and took Haney's arm. It confirmed what she'd expected, Sue and Haney would be getting married soon too.

The Registrar's office staff, who issued the burial permits, presented Marcia with a gift as she passed them.

"You girls look incredible, congratulations Marcia." said the Deputy Registrar.

The photographer took as many pictures as he could of the congratulatory handshakes and hugs. Outside City Hall, near the fountain, they assembled for photos. Some of the office staff slipped out and snapped pictures of the wedding party with their cellphones.

"I wasn't expecting that," said a breathless Marcia. "Did you arrange that Ryan?"

"No, it caught me off guard too. Jim?"

"Not me sir," replied a happy Jim. "You're well-liked and respected. It stands to reason the word of your marriage would get out. It's not easy to keep a secret at City Hall."

As Jim went to get the car, Jennifer moved over to Marcia. "What a lovely, simple ceremony that was. Can I see your ring?"

Marcia pulled off her glove and extended her hand. The band was slender and plain, Marcia had slipped her engagement ring on as well. The set was beautifully matched and it suited her. As Jim pulled the car up one of the parking authority officers approached him with a slip of paper. Jim laughed, accepted it and slapped the officer on the arm.

"VIP parking for the rest of the day," said Jim as he opened the doors for Marcia and Jennifer. We'll be able to park right at the falls."

The wedding lunch was held in a private room at one of the big hotels. Candlelight and flowers gave the room a romantic glow. Jim opened the champagne that was chilling at the table and poured everyone a glass. Jennifer rose for her speech first.

"To Ryan and Marcia, may the years be as kind to you as you are to each other now, may your wealth be in love and not just riches. Agree to disagree when you don't see eye to eye. Always kiss each other goodbye. May you laugh long and live long." She raised her glass and they had a solemn toast.

Jim rose and cleared his throat. "I don't think I can top that, Jennifer." He turned to Ryan. "Ryan, you are my best friend. We've been through some battles, you and I and I am truly honoured to be your best man. Marcia, Ryan waited a long time for you, and you have exceeded his expectations. He is a lucky man. Ryan—my best advice to you, now that you're a husband. Share everything with your wife, including the housework."

The four of them burst out laughing. Ryan's reputation as a neat freak was well known.

Jim raised his glass. "To Mr. and Mrs. Gillespie." They clinked their glasses. "Before I sit down, Jennifer and I know you're both beach bums, so no Vegas trips for you. When you can both get away, enjoy your honeymoon." Jim started to hand the envelope to Ryan, then pulled back and gave it Marcia. "I'd better give this to the boss," he said and more laughter filled the room. Marcia looked at Ryan and opened the card with the cheque. They read it together. Marcia stood, walked around the table, and gave a surprised Jim a kiss on the cheek and a hug. She swept Jennifer up in a hug as well, tears brimming her eyes.

"Thank you both. We were not expecting this."

Ryan spoke up, "Yes, you two, thank you. Rest assured, as we take this trip, making memories that will last our lifetime, we'll remember your generosity." He leaned over and kissed Jennifer on the cheek and shook Jim's hand, then hugged him. *And to think, a little over twenty-four hours ago he was yelling at me. Now I get a kiss.* Her mind drifted back to the first time she saw Detective Sergeant Gillespie and was taken with his blue eyes and crooked grin. She smiled at Marcia, who reciprocated. It was the perfect outcome.

After a lunch filled with much laughter and merriment and good-natured teasing, they left to go to the falls for pictures. Jim was delighted with the VIP parking pass. The afternoon sun cast a perfect light. The local photographer, skilled at making the best use of Niagara Falls, posed the four of them in several spots before doing the couple's photos. A few tourists stopped to take pictures of the wedding party as well.

Jennifer walked away from Ryan and Marcia as the photographer finished the group picture and photographed the two lovebirds. Jim followed beside her. She stretched and turned her face into to the cold mist rising from the Horseshoe Falls.

"How's your new job?" she asked. He rested his arms on the railing and stared at the rushing water.

"Challenging, interesting, much different than being a police officer. It was a good move for me." He started to say more, but stopped himself.

"What is it?" Jennifer touched his arm gently.

"Ask me later," he said, smiling down at her. He turned around and looked at the few tourists walking up and down the parkway. Jennifer followed suit, sitting on the edge of the barrier.

There was a person standing some distance from them, watching. The face looked familiar. Jennifer, caught off guard, stared for a minute, then turned to Jim.

"Do you still have Sue's work number?"

"Yes, I do, why?"

"Call her and tell her Agnes is watching Ryan and Marcia. Give her the location. I'm going to speak to her."

"Wait!" Jim was too late. Jennifer started toward Agnes. As she approached, she put a bright smile on her face. Agnes was staring at Marcia and Ryan, a strange look on her face. Jennifer slowed down and approached Agnes carefully. She was a few feet away when Agnes snapped out of her revere and noticed her.

"Hi Agnes."

A flicker of fear crossed Agnes' face, the same flash of fear Jennifer had noticed when she asked Agnes to tie the knot on Grimsby's hammock.

"They make a great couple, don't they?"

Agnes didn't answer. Jennifer's mind raced. She wasn't sure what to say next.

"I didn't get a chance to thank you." It sounded lame. "The kitchen, it's perfect. It exceeded my expectations."

"Oh. You're welcome." There was a long pause. *Now what? If she gets away, you could be charged with interfering. Why didn't you think before you acted?*

"Carol told me you quit. I was sorry to hear that. Was it because Graham was gone?"

"I couldn't work with Carol. I didn't kill Graham. I loved him. Carol did it, she killed him."

"I don't understand. Carol was cleared of all charges. She was released because she had an alibi."

"Exactly," she spat back. "When I went back to the shop that night, he was already dead. It wasn't me."

"Did you see Carol there?"

"No." She paused. "There was a white car

parked out back in Graham's spot."

"You said you loved Graham."

Agnes began twisting the tie on her coat over and over. "He used me," she whimpered. "I got his drugs and paid for them when he didn't have any money. He was upset with Carol. I told him to forget her. I told him I loved him and would take care of him, and he turned on me." She started to sniffle.

"Agnes, if it wasn't Carol, and it wasn't you, then who do you think killed Graham?"

"I don't know. It wasn't me."

"How did Carol's tape, tied with that neat knot you do, get around his neck?"

"I don't know. I was mad earlier when he called me names and said he didn't love me. But he was already dead when I found him."

"Did you tell the police about the white car?"

"I didn't tell the police nothing. I don't have to. I didn't do it."

Jennifer could see Jim standing about fifteen feet away, behind Agnes. He gave Jennifer a brief nod. She decided to rephrase her question.

"Agnes, why did you tie Carol's tape around his neck?"

"I didn't. I keep *telling* you that. He loved Carol, he kept saying he loved her. He should have been

242

mine. I hate her. I want her in jail. I never want to see her again."

"That's why you quit?"

"Of course, I couldn't work with her knowing he loved her." A lone tear trickled down her cheek. "Look at those two." She waved her hand in the direction of Marcia and Ryan. "That should be me." She looked at Jennifer defiantly.

"No one deserves to be mistreated, Agnes."

She looked at Jennifer, and without another word, turned to go.

"Agnes."

She turned back to Jennifer. "What?"

"Did you take Graham to the cemetery?"

Agnes nodded.

"Why?"

"I heard you on the phone telling the cemetery to prepare a grave. I decided Graham needed to be buried, so I took him to the cemetery. There are lots of graves there, I found one that was empty and put him in it. I have to go now." Agnes turned to leave.

A squad car pulled up to the side of the boulevard beside Agnes. Jennifer felt bad for the unhappy woman. She could see two officers get out and start toward her.

"Agnes, the police have been looking for you.

Tell them the truth. I want to believe you didn't kill Graham. Tell them what you told me."

Agnes looked back over her shoulder and then walked toward the policemen, her shoulder's slumped in defeat. They greeted her respectfully and she walked to the squad car between them. Jim walked over to her as Ryan came up behind her.

"What's going on?" Ryan asked.

"Agnes was watching the two of you. Jim called the station."

Ryan opened his mouth to say something. A look from Jim caused him to snap it shut.

"Photo's done?" asked Jim.

"They are," said Ryan as he turned back to Marcia and took her arm. "We can't thank you both enough, it was a perfect day."

Jim looked at Marcia. "Ready?"

"I'm ready."

"Then let's get you to your car."

Jim took Jennifer's arm and lagged back a bit behind Ryan and Marcia.

"I've got your back. Good work. We'll talk later."

"Thanks."

After they sent Marcia and Ryan off for their northern getaway, Jim opened the car door for

244

Jennifer and got into the driver's seat.

"What now kiddo?"

"What would you like to do?"

"I asked first."

Jennifer chuckled. "Would you like to stop for a few groceries, have a drink, a bite to eat at my place, see my new kitchen, tell me what you almost told me earlier today, discuss Agnes, or meet my twin?

"Hmm, tough one. How about all of the above."

"We're going to be quite the pair at the grocery store. This should be fun."

Sure enough, they turned more than a few heads as they picked up groceries. Jim and Jennifer had fun *hunting and gathering* in their finery, as Jim put it. A gentle dance song started playing over the speakers and Jim took her hand, pushed the cart down the aisle and the two of them waltzed, laughing happily. A few shoppers stopped to watch, then applauded as they finished.

It took two trips up the stairs at the funeral home, each, to bring in all the groceries. Jim helped put things away, then sat down and looked around.

"I love what you've done with the place, if I may be a bit cliché," he said. "It's warm and inviting."

"Glad you like it. My first order of business is a

cup of tea. Then, I am going to make a batch of cookies."

"Sounds perfect." Jim sighed. "It seems like a long time ago when you last served cookies and tea, in reality, it's only been a few months. How've you been coping? Does the kidnapping still haunt you?"

"It's fading a bit. I still have panic attacks. Ryan said the preliminary hearing is coming up, I hope the Crown doesn't need me there."

"They shouldn't. Ryan makes sure the team has all their ducks in a row before submitting evidence. If they do, give me a call, I'll walk you through the process and provide some moral support."

"Thanks." She puttered around the kitchen, put the hot water in the teapot, then pulled some fresh bakery cookies they had purchased and put them on a plate.

"These should do until I get the others baked." She pulled out her china mugs and set them on the island. Jim moved to one of the island chairs to continue chatting while she worked. But Jennifer wasn't going to let him get off that easy.

"Now, my turn. What were you going to say to me earlier?"

"I was going to say that you have an admirer in my boss. Mr. Wisener was asking about you yesterday." Jim picked up a cookie and groaned with pleasure as he took a bite.

"John has been more than kind to me. I'm fond of him too, maybe a little too much so." She could feel the colour rise in her cheeks as she admitted to Jim what she had been afraid to admit completely to herself. She felt safe with Jim, she knew he wouldn't judge her for her feelings toward Mr. Wisener.

"You're an old soul, wise beyond your years. Age is only a number."

"It's not that, I agree with you there, it's our lifestyles. I could not, would not, want to live in that kind of luxury. It's a bubble. I need to be here, this is what I want to do with my life. It would never work." It was time to change the subject. She poured their tea and sat at the corner of the island.

"Anne should be here soon. You'll like her. She's blunt and forthright and a bit of a steamroller at times. She has a genius IQ and doesn't do stupid. I'll make sure she gets something to eat, that should stop her growling at us, then you two will probably talk half the night. She matches your intellect."

Jim's eyebrow went up. "Is she as stubborn as you?"

"Exponentially more."

His infectious laugh filled the room. "When do

you have to get back to work?"

"Tuesday. You?"

"Midnight tonight. I'm on call this weekend and I'll be available if Gordon needs an extra pair of hands at Williams."

Jim took a sip of his tea and, raising an eyebrow, looked at her thoughtfully. "All work and no play..."

She was about to respond when her phone rang. Anne had arrived.

"Garage door is open, Elaine is in the front office, she wants to say hi to you. Come on up when you're done."

She heard Anne coming up the stairs ten minutes later. Grimsby heard her footsteps and bounded off the back of the couch and went to the door to greet her. Anne closed the door behind her and stared down at him. He looked up at her as he sat at her feet.

Jim chuckled. "Mexican stand-off," he muttered to Jennifer.

Anne caved first. "Hello Grimsby," she said bluntly. That was enough for Grimsby, she'd acknowledged him. He returned to his spot on the couch and watched her every move as she put her suitcase in the spare room and hung her coat up.

"Tea?"

"Yes, please," responded her twin. Anne stared at Jennifer, her face expressionless. "You look nice."

"I'll take nice. Anne, this is Jim." The two of them shook hands as Jennifer poured Anne's tea and pushed the plate with the few remaining cookies toward her. "I'll leave you two to get acquainted, I'm going to get changed."

Five minutes later, after she'd put on her jeans and a sweater and before she scrubbed the makeup from her face, she paused, taking a long look herself as a different person. She had enjoyed being pretty for the day. She returned to the kitchen to find Anne and Jim in an intense discussion about the various forms of proportional representation vs. first past the post voting. They argued back and forth while Jennifer made fresh cookies, then started dinner. The steaks were almost cooked before the heated discussion settled down into a more amicable one.

"To hear you two squabble you'd think you were on opposite sides," Jennifer said as she laid out the place settings. "In reality, you both agree on most of what you were discussing, at least I think you do."

"We're going to have to talk about whether or not Senators should be elected after dinner," said Anne, giving Jim a look that said *bring it on.*

"That's a hot topic." Jim grinned. He was clearly enjoying sparring with Anne.

"Dinner's not going stay hot if you two don't eat," Jennifer said pleasantly. She was delighted to see Anne and Jim engaged in a tete-a-tete. Anne could be intense at times and she'd clearly met her match with Jim.

After a pleasant dinner discussing Ryan and Marcia's wedding, Anne and Jim continued their bantering over dishes and clean up. Jennifer curled up in her chair with a book, half-listening to the details of their political discourse. She was happy to be outside the discussion, it had been a long day and she was disturbed by her discussion with Agnes, who appeared to her to be emotionally unstable. Gordon called once, apologizing profusely for disturbing her. He'd received a call from the police asking him to attend a coroner's call and he wasn't sure what to do.

"Is Jeff going with you?"

"I wasn't sure if I should call him or you," was the response.

"Call Jeff," Jennifer said. "Never do a coroner's call alone. Each van is stocked with the equipment necessary for precautionary measures, along with extra coveralls, masks, face shields and gloves. If he isn't available, then you work your way up the pecking order, so to speak. Where's the call?"

"On the highway, MVA they said."

"OK, get a hold of Jeff pronto. Once we receive a call it means they need the body removed quickly. The police and fire and ambulance personnel have done their job and the coroner has given permission to clear the scene. We try to respond within half an hour of the call, it's courtesy. Some of the first responders may have been there for hours and we don't wish to hold them up or disrespect the deceased by being late. You might want to swing by and pick up Jeff after you have called him, it'll save time."

"OK." Gordon sounded a little tentative in his response.

"Don't worry, you'll be fine. Let Jeff take the lead. It'll be second nature to you in no time."

With a tiny sigh of what Jennifer hoped was relief and a "thank you", Gordon signed off. Jennifer immediately sent Jeff a text.

"CC, new to G, take lead. He will pick you up."

Seconds later Jeff responded.

"Got it."

Marcia had taught him well. The staff could not text words like coroners call or homicide, Jennifer felt it was inappropriate. As part of staff training, she made it clear they were always representing the funeral home. There was a risk of someone seeing what they were texting when they were out in public.

"Would you like a drink Jennifer?" Jim asked on his way to the fridge.

"A beer please. Gordon and Jeff are off on a coroner's call, it looks like I can relax a bit and man the phones." Jim prepared her drink and moved to the living area. Anne following behind with her beverage, picking up the conversation with Jim again. By eleven o'clock, Jennifer rose and announced she was going to bed.

"Good night," was the response in unison from the other two. They didn't even look up as they continued their discussion, both of them leaning forward in their chairs, intensely engaged.

Waking with the morning sun, Jennifer rose refreshed, hoping it would be a quiet weekend so she and Anne could have some time together. She knew Anne wouldn't be up for hours, so she silently went about her morning routine before settling at the island in her kitchen drinking her coffee. Elaine was off for the weekend and as she rose to go downstairs to open up for the day, she heard footsteps, then a key in the lock. Anne bounded through the door, energetic and looking rather pleased with herself.

"You're are up early," Jennifer said to her twin.

"Haven't been to bed yet."

"What? Why?"

"Jim and I took the wedding car back to the place where you rent your limos, then we went out for a coffee and had a nice long walk. He's going to pick me up around two this afternoon. If you haven't seen me by one-thirty, wake me up will ya? We're going to the conservatory to look at the flowers, have dinner, maybe take in a movie, go for another walk. Do you want to come with us?"

Jennifer looked at Anne with considerable skepticism. "Where is my twin sister? What did you do to her?"

Anne laughed. "I thought I'd be bored hanging around here if you were working. Guess not. Jim's off till Tuesday, so am I. He has a bit of time off over Christmas next week, so do I. He offered to come to Ottawa. That should be fun. Anyway, I'm going to shower and grab some sleep. See you later."

Humming softly to herself, Anne disappeared into the spare bedroom. Jennifer shook her head in disbelief and quietly shut the door behind her as she went downstairs. So much for her visit with her twin.

Minutes after going downstairs the phone rang with a first call. The family was able to come in right away and the consultation went smoothly.

After they left, she prepared the file and did the transfer. Time passed quickly. Jennifer realized she'd forgotten to wake up Anne. It was hard getting Anne to wake up, let alone get up at all. She could be a real bear. It was 1:50 p.m. She had ten minutes to get ready.

"Shoot," muttered Jennifer. "Anne's not going to be impressed."

The front door of the funeral home opened as she started down the hallway. She did a three-sixty and went back to the lobby to see who was there. It was Jim.

"Hey kiddo, how's it going?"

"Great Jim, you?"

"No complaints. Is your super sibling up yet?"

"I am," said a familiar voice from the hall. Jennifer turned to her sister. Anne was nicely dressed, her hair and makeup perfect. Better yet, she was smiling. Anne hoarded smiles, releasing them only when necessary, rarely "just because".

"Good morning, Jim."

"Good afternoon. You look lovely. All set?"

"Are you going to join us for dinner?" Anne looked at her expectantly.

"No, I've got work to do. Thanks, though."

"All right—see you later." She watched Anne laughing as Jim held the car door for her, the two of them already engaged in conversation.

Jennifer turned to go to the prep room. *It's been a long time since I've seen Anne this happy and carefree. I'd never have thought Jim and Anne would have that much in common.*

After completing the prep she wandered into the new suite, sat in one of the chairs, pulled out her phone and checked on Gordon. He also had a call, a direct cremation and had completed the file. Jennifer chatted with him for a few minutes, reminding him to call if he needed her. She sat and thought about Marcia and Ryan and their first day as a married couple, before going to the prep room to finish dressing the body.

She turned on the radio and tuned it to a fifty's station, singing as she worked, relishing the peace and quiet of the Saturday afternoon. After locking up the funeral home for the day she went upstairs, fed Grimsby, and made dinner. A coroner's call came in just as she was sitting down to supper. After getting the details and address, she called Jeff and asked him to meet her downstairs.

"On my way," was his cheerful response.

Disconnecting, she looked at her dinner. Sometimes coroner's calls took hours—the police call prematurely, the coroner was running late... She was too hungry to wait. She picked up her fork and shovelled the food in, finishing her meal in four minutes. Belching contentedly, she grabbed her coat and went down to double-check the supplies in the van.

It was a house call. The resident had died days before. No one had entered or left the home until the police were called. Jennifer quickly regretted eating. After donning protective gear, they collapsed the stretcher and opened the body bag. The officer asked their permission to step outside for a smoke.

Together she and Jeff moved some of the furniture. The heat and smell were getting to her. She could feel her face getting hot.

"I wolfed down supper," she said quietly to Jeff.

"That wasn't smart. You of all people should know better. If it's any consolation, I did the same thing once. Had to run outside. I got sick and threw up in the bushes. Talk about embarrassing." Jeff grinned at her.

"Were you with Brent?" she asked, breathing

slowly through her mouth, doing her best to concentrate on the task at hand.

"Nope. Marcia." He chuckled. "She was nice about it. I thought she might be mad at me. Which reminds me, how was the wedding?"

Jennifer appreciated Jeff's attempts to distract her from the rising nausea. "Marcia was beautiful. I'm sure you'll see the pictures at some point. Remind me to show you the one's I have on my phone. Ryan looked handsome and distinguished too. We had a great day."

Having completed their prep, Jeff moved over to the other side of the body. "Ready?"

Jennifer nodded.

"On three," he said and counted it down.

Unfortunately, the decomposition was a bit more advanced than they'd realized. Jeff's gloves slipped in some exposed adipose tissue and the body landed on the stretcher with a thump. The expelled gas and air was noxious. It was too much for Jennifer. Ripping off her mask she made a beeline for the bathroom, making it to the sink in the nick of time. She continued retching for a few minutes. Shaky and sweaty, she hung onto the sink, willing herself not to pass out. Once the worst was over, she found some cleaner under the sink and scrubbed it.

Ten minutes after her dash to the bathroom she emerged, looking a bit worse for wear.

She found Jeff in the kitchen chatting amicably with the police officer.

"Feeling better?" he asked kindly.

She nodded. "I'm sorry. It's been a while since I've that happen at a scene."

"Yeah, well, you aren't the first," the officer said. "I beat you to it. When I first arrived, the smell was so bad you could hardly stand it coming up the walk. I lost my lunch. I hate this kind of call. I'd rather be doing traffic duty. How you guys do this time after time is a mystery to me."

Jennifer's smile was a little weak. "I don't think one ever gets used to these calls. It's bad enough a person dies alone and isn't missed for days. These transfers can be a bit of a challenge."

"The Coroner showed up, got halfway up the walk and stopped. He wouldn't come in, he pronounced the death from there. Of course, that meant I had to check for foul play, in case it wasn't natural causes. That's how I lost my lunch."

Jennifer shook her head, disgusted. "That happened to my partner and I once in Toronto, the Coroner would not come in. He scribbled a diagnosis, handed me the death certificate and left.

My partner and I found a stab wound. The Coroner made it back in record time. He could have lost his appointment over that. It's not your job, or mine to determine the cause of death."

"True. Fortunately, the majority go out of their way to get to the scene within a reasonable time and most do their job. You guys need a hand getting to the van?"

"The stretcher is in the front hall, the furniture is back in place," Jeff said to Jennifer. "Let the man go home." He turned to the officer. "Thanks for the help. I enjoyed our chat."

"You're most welcome. You guys have a great night."

Once the van was loaded, Jennifer sat back in the passenger seat and let Jeff drive. She closed her eyes for a few minutes, enjoying the cooler air in the van. Jeff had not turned the heat on, it would only disperse the smell.

"You know," she said thoughtfully. "You've come such a long way. I'm impressed with your people skills."

"How so?"

"You get along with everyone. You and Marcia are such fun together, yet you show her complete respect as your boss. You bonded well with the officer and made him feel good about his job. You asked how I was feeling after I was sick. Not too bad for a young guy. You have empathy and insight and you read people well. All valuable skills to have."

"Aww, thanks. My mom might differ, but although it may not seem like it sometimes, she raised me well."

After they placed the deceased in the morgue, Jeff dropped her off. There was no sign of Anne or Jim. Together they put the van in the garage and Jennifer replenished the supplies.

"Here are a few pictures of the wedding," she said as she pulled out her phone and handed it to Jeff. He whistled, clearly impressed at Marcia's appearance.

"She looks fabulous, I barely recognized her."

"Do you and Gordon need a hand tomorrow?" she asked.

"Desta's working. I'll tell Gordon you asked. I think we should be OK though." He took one last look at the pictures before handing back her phone.

"In that case, let's hope the rest of the night is quiet. Take care."

Jennifer locked the door behind him and trundled up the stairs. She was getting hungry again and fixed herself a snack. She and Grimsby curled up together while she read.

It was after eleven when she had her bath and went to bed. She lay awake thinking about Agnes's comments. What if she was telling the truth? After muddling it over and not coming up with an answer, her last thoughts before she fell asleep were of Anne and Jim, wondering what they were up to.

14

Anne's door was closed when Jennifer went quietly down the stairs Sunday morning. She hadn't heard her come in. Sundays were usually days to catch up on files and bills and she worked at her computer, getting up a few times to stretch and get coffee.

At noon a family came in to inquire about pricing. It was the family of the gentleman she and Jeff had transferred last evening. She took her time with them, doing her best to make them feel comfortable. They were understandably upset that their dad had not been found sooner, and they blamed themselves for not staying in touch.

"Is there any way we'll be able to see him?" asked the daughter, a well-dressed young woman who worked in the financial district of Toronto.

Jennifer was careful with her answer. She could not deny them the right to see their father, on the other hand, it might not be a positive experience for them. She did her best to confront them with the reality without traumatizing or offending them.

"I transferred your father to the hospital morgue last night. Unfortunately, he'd been dead for a while before his neighbour went to check on him. He is not in good condition. It would not be wise to have an open casket."

"Why?" asked her brother. "The police said they thought he'd only been dead five days. That shouldn't matter, wouldn't embalming fix it?"

Jennifer took a deep breath. "Certain factors influence decomposition, such as temperature or location. Your dad was in a heated home, which was sealed."

"So?" prompted the brother.

"Once we die, our bodies immediately start the work of decomposition." His sister flinched. "The heat accelerated that process."

"How bad?" The brother wouldn't let it go. He wanted to know, so she gave him a simplistic response.

"It was bad enough that we wore protective gear. Essentially there are three stages that occur with decomposition. The first stage is autolysis, the cells in the body stop working at the time of death and begin to break down. In Stage Two the bacteria in the body starts to break down the tissues and Stage

Three is the final and longest breakdown stage." She wondered if she had given them too much information. It was one thing to discuss it clinically with a co-worker, it was another to talk to a family member about someone they loved decomposing in stages.

"Maybe we should go with direct cremation," suggested the daughter.

"Maybe. What stage was he?" asked the son.

"It's safe to say he was in Stage Three, which is why I don't recommend viewing."

"I need to see him," he replied.

Having given the family the facts, Jennifer knew she had to grant their wish.

"Then you should. I suggest we meet at the hospital. I can make arrangements to have a chaplain meet us outside the morgue. Would that work for you?"

The siblings looked at each other and nodded. "We both have to be back in Toronto by morning for work."

"If you'll excuse me for a few minutes, I'll call the hospital. Why don't you follow me to the lounge and have a coffee or tea while you wait?

"I could use a tea, thanks," said the daughter.

Jennifer went into her office and closed the door,

pleased that it was now soundproofed. She dialed the chaplain's department at the hospital. Chaplain Regina Salinas answered.

After exchanging the usual pleasantries, Jennifer got down to business.

"I have a brother and sister who'd like to view their father. Jeff and I did the coroner's call last night. The body is in decomposition. Are you available to facilitate them this afternoon?

"I've never attended a morgue visit before, although I'm happy to help. Do you think it's a good idea for them to see their dad?"

"It's not my job to tell them what to do. I gave them the facts and options, they chose to view him. They have to be back in Toronto by tomorrow and it's a direct cremation. Normally I'd bring him to the funeral home and let them see him there, but the crematorium is closed on Sunday and I'd rather not leave him in the funeral home. The hospital morgue is temperature controlled."

"Fair enough," responded Regina. "Is half an hour acceptable?"

"Let me check."

She opened her door and went into the lounge.

"The Chaplain can meet us at the hospital in a half hour. I'll drive you over if you wish."

266

The two looked at each other.

"Are you sure?" asked the sister.

"I am," responded the brother. "You don't have too if it's too hard."

"You can decide when we get to the hospital," Jennifer said.

"All right." She returned to Regina and let her know they'd be there shortly. Returning to the lounge, she sat down on the edge of a chair, looking from the sister to the brother, then back again.

"Chaplain Salinas will meet us shortly. I'll warm up the car while you get your coats. Be right back."

She plucked her black wool overcoat from the coat rack in the garage and stepped outside. A blast of wintery blustering wind slammed her. Snow had started swirling in the cold wind and snatched her breath away.

"Wow," she muttered. "When did that happen?" An avid weather watcher, she realized she hadn't checked the forecast for the second time in a month. Wrapping her coat around her she was happy to be sheltered from the wind as she got into the freezing car. She started it up, set the heat and held tight to the door as she left the vehicle to go back inside. The wind snatched it from her hand, threatening to take it off its hinges. She noticed Anne's rental car at the back of the lot, snow on the windshield.

She must be upstairs. I'll have to run up and visit for a bit when I get back.

Entering the garage, Jennifer stamped the snow off her shoes and sought out the family.

"I'll pick you up at the front door," she said. "It's a bit blustery, so wait until I pull up."

On the way to the hospital, Jennifer talked with the siblings about their work in Toronto and compared some familiar spots, including a restaurant she liked. Once she arrived at the hospital she pulled up front, let them out and then parked around back at the morgue. She texted Chaplain Regina to let her know they had arrived, and what colour of shirt the son wore she could find them.

Cutting through the back of the hospital to the front, she stopped at the Admitting desk to sign for the morgue key. When she arrived in the lobby, Chaplain Regina was chatting with the family. Jennifer gave them time to acclimate, and waited for the chaplain's nod before led the way to the pathology department.

"If you wouldn't mind waiting for a minute with the chaplain, I'll go and get your father." They nodded solemnly. She knew Regina would give them the opportunity to change their mind. The somber surroundings were a deterrent enough.

She double-gloved, masked and prepared herself for the odorous assault. It made her eyes water. Pulling some extra gloves and masks from the box by the door, she slipped them in her pocket. After unzipping the body bag, her breathing became shallow as the odor assaulted her. The father was still in the same position he had been when she and Jeff dropped him off. Tucking the sheet that she and Jeff had used at the scene under his chin a little tighter, Jennifer zipped up the body bag so just his head showed. She then covered his entire body with a clean sheet from one of the shelves in the cooler. Pushing the stretcher to the door, she slipped out alone.

"Here are some gloves and masks for you. Are you sure you wish to proceed?"

The brother nodded, his sister looked like a deer in the headlights.

"Chaplain?" Regina nodded.

Once everyone was masked and gloved Jennifer opened the morgue door and slowly pushed the stretcher into the hallway, then gently moved the fresh sheet she'd placed over him away from his face.

For a minute, time stood still, the family frozen

269

to the spot. Regina didn't move either. Jennifer stepped back and waited.

The sister stared at her father, shock and horror reflecting in her eyes. She tore off the mask and gloves and ran from the hallway. Regina followed, dropping her mask and gloves on the floor for Jennifer to pick up and put in the biohazard box. Her brother moved closer to his father's puffy, mottled face. He tentatively reached out, touched his father's cheek and whispered softly.

"Bye dad. Love you." Tears spilled from his eyes and slid under the mask. He sighed deeply. "OK," he said, stepping back and removing his mask and gloves. Jennifer held out her hand to receive them.

He waited down the hall a bit, leaning up against the wall while Jennifer tidied up and put his dad back into the morgue cooler.

"Thank you," he said as they walked down the hall together. "I needed to see him."

"I understand. I would be the same."

The conversation on the way back to the funeral home was minimal as the siblings discussed what else needed to be done before they drove back to Toronto.

As Jennifer gave them the final information

about the cremation, the brother asked if she knew the solicitor who was serving as executor. "His name is Duncan."

"I do," she replied. "He's a man of integrity and kindness. You are in good hands."

She shook both their hands as they left and then she went upstairs for a quick lunch. Anne's door was closed. She looked around. Her coat was gone.

"Grimsby, have you seen Anne today?" Grimsby yawned and looked at her through sleepy eyes. "Oh well, maybe we can visit tonight." It looked like it was going to be a long, quiet afternoon. There were times when the term "deathly quiet" seemed appropriate in the funeral home. She did her best to recall her conversation with Agnes at the falls and realized that not once had Agnes said she'd tied that knot or killed Graham. *But it had to be her. No one just takes a body to the cemetery because it's there.*

Sunday traffic was minimal on both streets, the snow muted noise. There wasn't a sound. *All I need is a good mystery, a cup of tea and a ticking clock. I wonder if I should call Anne.* She decided against it. Anne was obviously having a good time with Jim. They didn't need a third person hanging around. The afternoon and evening stretched on, with no word from her sister and she still wasn't home by the time Jennifer went to bed—and she didn't hear her come in either.

She rose early Monday and double-checked the paperwork on the cremation. It took a while to drive to the crematorium, the road was snow-covered and the wind whipped it up, causing whiteouts. She drove carefully, speed could be deadly with such weather conditions.

The round-trip took nearly three hours and she was glad to be back safe. The van wasn't the most stable vehicle for winter driving, even with snow tires. There was a car in the lot when she returned. She found Jim and Anne and Elaine chatting in the lounge.

"Hello strangers," she said to Jim and Anne.

Jim grinned as he and Anne exchanged glances.

"Guess we haven't been around much," Anne said. "So Jim suggested we come by and visit for a bit, that is, if you have time."

"I do, and I'm glad you did. What on earth have the two of you been up to?"

"We've had a great time. Jim's hotel room overlooks the falls, it is cozy and pleasant. He taught me how to play blackjack, so we went back to the casino a couple of times. We did the Bird Kingdom, loved it, and the Butterfly Conservatory." Anne paused to catch her breath before she continued. "Mostly we talked."

"I didn't hear you come in. "And I didn't hear you leave."

Anne raised an eyebrow and gave her twin a *are you seriously that dumb* kind of look. "That's because I haven't been here since we left Saturday, except to pick up my suitcase. You were sleeping."

The look on Jennifer's face made even Elaine laugh.

"You mean to tell me you didn't notice the fridge hadn't been raided, my coat wasn't there, my car hadn't moved? I love you dearly Jen, but you really do need to get a life. All you do is work and hide in your apartment."

For a few seconds, her sister's remark stung a bit before she realized Anne was right. She hadn't noticed Anne's extended absence.

She started to chuckle, then laughed out loud. "Do you mean I tiptoed around all weekend for nothing? I can't believe I was that clueless."

"All work and no play..." reminded Jim dryly. "What are you doing this afternoon?"

"I should check with Brent, see if they need help

and I probably should..."

"Shhhh!" That came from Elaine. Jennifer looked at her, surprised.

"Go. Get out of here. I'll call you if I need you," she said.

"But..."

"Enough of the *shoulds*. Have some fun with your sister and Jim."

Jennifer looked at the three of them. She was tempted as she mulled it over.

"Where to?" she asked happily.

"Let's go to the casino and play a bit of blackjack," Anne suggested. "You've been trying to get me to learn how to play for years. Now I know how, and it's fun. We could have dinner."

"Let's have lunch first," said Jim. "I'm getting peckish."

"There's plenty upstairs. You can raid the fridge, I'll get changed. Come on Elaine, join us."

Grimsby greeted the noisy crew as they entered the apartment. As Jennifer changed to dress pants and a sweater, she sat on the edge of her bed listening to the merriment coming from the kitchen.

Marcia's wedding and Jim and Anne's visit should be a wake-up call for me to stop being so intense. Obviously, Anne isn't the only one who noticed. Jennifer used work sometimes to avoid socializing or relaxing. Anne was the same way. *At least we have that in common, although it's not always a good thing.*

Joining the group in the kitchen, they had lunch, then left for the casino. With the heavy snow, the traffic was light. Anne and Jim were ahead of her in Jim's car and she could see them talking, animated and happy. *I can't believe Anne and Jim spent the weekend together. I'm such a prude.*

The casino was busy and noisy. They found a table where the three of them could sit together and play for about an hour. Jennifer cashed out with almost double of what she'd brought, Jim did the best of the three of them, even Anne made a bit. They played slots for a while, then went to Tim Horton's for coffee.

"Jim's going to drive me to the airport tomorrow," Anne said. "I'll drop my rental car off here in town tomorrow morning."

"Are you staying with Jim tonight?" Jennifer was surprised at how casual that sounded. Anne and Jim were sitting shoulder to shoulder.

"Of course," was Anne's response. Jim nodded.

"Jim and I have had a few long talks about your kidnapping and his stabbing and PTSD," Anne said.

"It's given me an idea for an article. We can talk some more about it. I'll work on it and submit it to my editor." She looked at Jennifer intensely. "I know you see me as stiff and reclusive, that's my way of dealing with things. But you're no different. You work, then keep working, then hide in your apartment. Jim has helped me see how damaging my avoidance behaviour is." As Anne looked up at Jim, he smiled down at her, Jennifer realized with a start that they'd become a couple.

It was too much to process immediately and her Scarlett O'Hara voice popped into her head. *I can't think about that right now, if I do I just know I'll go crazy. I'll think about it tomorrow.* She didn't feel like being an adult right now. Anne's revelation hit hard, she knew it was true. And it felt like she was losing her twin when she saw how Anne and Jim related to each other. Her first thought was to do the very thing Anne had mentioned, curl up in her apartment and hide.

"Hey!" Jim's voice broke through her reverie. "Want to go over to the arcade and play?"

She looked at him and thought about how he had it right. Jim had learned to balance his personal life and his work life. He had taught Ryan to do the same. They spent the rest of the afternoon laughing

276

and playing like teenagers before settling down to a quiet dinner.

Jim's infectious laugh was good for the soul. Anne's spirit was light and as they said goodbye later in the evening, she gave them both a big hug, her mind clearer than it had been had for a long time.

Marcia showed up for work early the next morning. Jennifer was waiting for her in the lounge, coffee ready, eager to hear about the honeymoon. Marcia was glowing with happiness as they hugged.

"How was your time up north?" Jennifer asked as she handed Marcia her coffee.

"Fabulous. The weather was perfect. We walked the trails in the woods, saw all kinds of winter birds, cardinals and jays mostly. Oh, we also saw a little fox. We skated, tobogganed and we tried cross-country skiing. Snowshoeing isn't my sport, I suck at it. The time flew by. How's it been here? Were you busy?"

"Up until yesterday. I didn't see Jim and Anne. They spent the weekend together. We finally got together yesterday afternoon."

"I guess I owe Ryan ten bucks, he called it."

Jennifer cocked her head, puzzled.

"He figured Anne and Jim would hit it off.

277

They're both very intelligent, intense at times, and love politics and news. I pooh-poohed it and the bet was on. How do you feel about the two of them together?"

"It was a shock. I'll get used to it. I'm happy for both of them, they are cute together, laughing and playing like kids. Jim will be spending Christmas in Ottawa."

Marcia's responded with a knowing smile.

"Ryan didn't talk about work once. I'm proud of him. Have you heard anything more about Agnes?"

"No. And it's bothering me. Agnes seemed frightened and lost when we talked at the falls. She swore she didn't kill Graham and I want to believe her but…"

"But what?" prompted Marcia.

"It's the knot. *She* tied that knot. I'm sure of it."

"You'll find out soon enough," Marcia said, then changed the subject. "Ryan and
I want to thank you again for the wedding gift. It gives us something to look forward to anytime we need to get away. I love the beach."

"Which makes you easy to buy for." Jennifer laughed. "A beach is the last place I would want to spend a vacation."

"What's on today's agenda?"

"A trip to the crematorium to pick up some cremated remains, other than that, nothing really unless we get a call. William's has one funeral today. Would you like to visit Sherri's shop and poke around? Elaine will be here."

"Oh, lets! You didn't get much time to explore the last time we were there."

As they had their coffee, Jennifer used the opportunity to ask Marcia if she wanted to become the training director for the two funeral homes.

"I'd love too. It is reaching the point where training isn't a self-directed option for the staff. And you know how I feel about ongoing education. The day I stop learning is the day I should quit this job."

"Me too, that is, I agree," responded Jennifer.

It was late afternoon when Elaine called. They had shopped, Jennifer had picked up some vintage jewellery "just because" at Sherri's, they had lunch out and did a few thrift shops.

"This is not something you will want to hear Jennifer," said Elaine. Her tone was serious. Jennifer looked for a place to sit down. She had a bad feeling something terrible had happened.

"Agnes' mother just called to make arrangements. Agnes died by suicide last night. Her mom will be in shortly."

Time stopped. She could hear Elaine's voice, but it didn't register. Marcia was at her side quickly.

Marcia took the phone from her hand, told Elaine they were on their way, and tapped it off.

"Tell me in the car," Marcia said as she pulled out her keys. "Your reaction tells me this is not good news."

The drive back to the funeral home was a blur. Jennifer told Marcia what had happened.

"Can you take this call with me, please? I don't think I can do it alone."

"Of course. How awful. Poor Agnes."

Elaine met them at the garage door, file ready. "I made you both a cup of tea."

Once they were seated, Jennifer found the words she felt she needed to say.

"I feel partly responsible. If—"

"If we hadn't tried to get her to do that knot and scare her into thinking we thought she was a killer, maybe she'd be alive now," Marcia finished Jennifer's thought.

"Where did she die? Jennifer asked.

Elaine shook her head no. "At home, apparently," Elaine said.

Marcia and Jennifer exchanged glances. Marcia was the first to ask the question. "If she was guilty, why would they have released her?"

"Bail?"

There was no time to continue speculating, the front door opened and Elaine went to meet Agnes' mom.

With heavy hearts, both funeral directors introduced themselves. Jennifer sat beside Delores, Agnes mother, who was alone. Marcia sat behind the desk and took the lead.

"I'm so sorry. This is a terrible time for you Mrs. Wilson."

"Call me Delores." She started to cry and reached for Jennifer's hand. Jennifer took the woman's hand in both hers, riddled with guilt, feeling like she'd be in tears herself shortly.

"What happened?" asked Jennifer softly. "I saw her Friday, at the falls. We talked for a while."

"The police arrested her on suspicion of the murder of that Graham character. He's all she talked about. I was so glad to see him gone. I hoped Agnes would forget him and move on with her life." She paused as her tears flowed freely.

When she was ready, she continued. "The police had no proof, it was all about a knot and they kept her half the night, then let her go." Delores shook her head in disgust. "She didn't say much when she got home, but I knew it had been hard on her." Delores looked at Marcia, still holding tight to Jennifer's hands.

"Agnes was a little slow, you know, not quite right in the head. She wasn't like her brothers, they were sharper. She did bad at school, except for numbers. She was real good at numbers. She didn't have any friends. She didn't talk much, it made her panic when people talked to her and she had to talk back."

Neither funeral director responded. Jennifer could not have felt worse for Delores or Agnes.

"She tried living on her own, but she just couldn't do it. She had a bedroom downstairs. She was so proud when she got her driver's license, it took her a long time and a lot of tries."

Marcia passed Delores the tissue box as the silence lingered. Eventually, Delores released Jennifer's hand, looked up again, and continued as she twisted a tissue into a little string.

"Agnes, she told me about you girls, how friendly you were, and how kind. She didn't get much kindness in her life. That Graham, he was a mean one. Carol wasn't much better, she made my Agnes feel like she was nothing." Her mother looked up at the ceiling and crossed herself. "She's at peace now." Jennifer fought back the sobs that threatened to erupt, guilt covering her like a blanket. The atmosphere in the room was heavy with sorrow.

Marcia took her time leading Delores through the arrangements for her daughter. It was obvious that Delores was in no position to pay for a fancy funeral, nor did she expect it. She wanted her daughter cremated and the ashes returned to her.

"Would you and your sons consider a chapel service here? There would be no charge, Agnes stepped up to finish the renovations when Carol was..." Jennifer hesitated, searching for the word. "Away."

"We don't have no minister."

"I know a Chaplain who would be available."

"The boys would like that, giving their sister a proper send-off. Agnes loved them boys. She and the boys used to sneak into the graveyard and play hide and seek for hours. Never saw much sense in it, but it was fun for them."

"If you'll excuse me, I'll see if I can reach the Chaplain. Marcia will discuss the cost of the cremation with you, the rest we will take care of. Agnes was a hard worker and her work here was excellent."

Closing the door quietly behind her, Jennifer

went to her office and sank into her chair, putting her head in her hands as wave after wave of regret washed over. How could she have not noticed Agnes' struggles with communication? Eventually she forced herself back to the task at hand and called the hospital. Chaplain Clive answered.

"Hi Chaplain, it's Jennifer."

"Well, if it isn't my favourite little lassie. What can I do for you, girl?"

Jennifer gave him the basic details about Agnes and her suicide. He agreed to do the service the next afternoon.

"Poor wee lass," he said. "Don't you worry, we will make sure she is honoured and remembered. See you tomorrow."

"Thank you very much, Chaplain Clive," she said sincerely. She knew he'd do his best for the little family and it gave her some comfort. Elaine had left a note on her desk before she went home: Agnes had been released, there was no autopsy.

Delores had taken the bus to the funeral home and Marcia told her she'd drive her home and pick her up for the service the next day.

After the two of them left, Jennifer locked up and went upstairs to seek out Grimsby. Marcia called after she'd dropped off Delores and they agreed to order flowers for the service.

"I'll call Blooms, they can put it on the credit card for the funeral home," she said. "That was hard, that poor mother."

"Poor Agnes," responded Jennifer. "I don't think I'll be able to forgive myself for not seeing clearly. After what her mom said, I don't think Agnes killed Graham. I think she did bury him, because in her mind, that was the right thing to do. How could we have been so wrong?"

"I don't know," said Marcia soberly. "I feel horrible too. I need to get home. I'll see you tomorrow, bright and early. If we get a call tonight, I'll call Jeff, OK? You need a little time to yourself."

"Agreed. See you tomorrow."

For a long time, Jennifer sat with Grimsby in her arms before going to the freezer and pulling out the ice cream she and Jim had purchased. It was candy cane and mint, a cheerful Christmas flavour. She got a spoon, opened the lid and started eating mindlessly. Christmas was less than a week away and once again, her job had snatched the joy that most people found at that time of year. Added to that was the guilt she felt for not noticing Agnes' struggles.

Eventually, she put the little bit of ice cream

remaining in the freezer and watched TV, her mind not on the program, but on Delores and Agnes. She went to bed convinced she'd made a terrible mistake blaming Agnes for the murder.

15

Chaplain Clive met Marcia and Jennifer well before the service, then chatted quietly with Jennifer as Marcia went to pick up Agnes' mom and her brothers. He sensed the two funeral directors were grieving too, and he asked them to sit through the service.

The flowers on the casket and the bouquets at the side were yellow and white. Delores cried when she saw them. Elaine sat with Marcia and Jennifer at the back of the chapel. Simply and kindly Chaplain Clive led them through Agnes' life, the ups and downs, ending on a gentle note by explaining that Agnes had touched others in a profound way. He looked at Marcia and Jennifer as he said those words. There was no rush to leave, the family lingered in the chapel after Chaplain Clive finished. When they emerged, Delores swept Jennifer into a hug.

"Thank you for giving our girl such a fine send-off," she said. "Come on boys." Both of Agnes brothers shook Jennifer's hand and helped their mother into her coat. Marcia drove them home, leaving Jennifer with Chaplain Clive.

"Well, lassie, that service was hard on you, wasn't it?"

"They all are," she replied. "Some more than others."

"Aye, I have the same problem, I do." He fetched his coat and gloves. "Merry Christmas to you."

"You too, Chaplain," she said and hugged him firmly.

As his car pulled out of the parking lot, she sat down in the office across from Elaine.

"I was wrong, so horribly wrong about Agnes."

"We all were," responded Elaine. "I thought at first that Carol had killed Graham, then I figured it was Agnes. Now I don't have a clue who might have killed him."

Jennifer's phone rang, her call display indicated it was Ryan. She looked up at Elaine and shrugged. Maybe Marcia still had her cell phone off.

"Would you mind coming to the station for a quick chat?"

"Is something wrong?" Jennifer's stomach clenched. She hoped he wasn't going to confront her about her chat with Agnes.

"We can talk here."

"I'll see you shortly." She hung up and frowned as she looked at Elaine.

"I have to go down to the station. Maybe Jeff could take Agnes to the crematorium?"

"Marcia and I can manage, we'll see you later."

Upon arriving at the police station for once she didn't have to sit and wait, Sue immediately ushered her in.

"How are things?" she asked pleasantly.

"It's almost Christmas. It's a busy time for funeral directors. No exception this year. It's a bad time to lose someone." She realized that sounded a bit blunt, but she wasn't her usually cheery self.

She took her usual seat at the end of the table. Ryan also greeted her before he got down to business.

"This is for you. It was lying on Agnes coat near the door of her room." He handed her a sealed envelope with her first name and Spencer F. H. beneath it. "I'd like you to read it."

Without a word and feeling some trepidation, she slipped her finger under the flap and tore carefully along the top of the envelope and pulled out a single, folded page. It was written in a childish scrawl.

GRAVE MISTAKE

Jenifer:

U were nice 2 me. Not 2 many peeple were. I dont like peeple much.

I loved Graham. I thot he was charming. He was handsome & I wanted 2 be with him all the time.

4 2 years I showd him how much I loved him, I wood have done anything for him. I sold drugs 2 get money 4 him. Ur friend Travis taught me how. Graham talked about Carol all the time. I thot if he new I loved him, he wood 4get about her. When I told him I luved him Graham laughed in my face. He called me a cow and other bad things.

I told u I hated Carol. I did not hate her all the time, I just wanted 2 be like her. She had a man who lovd her. I saw them 2gether once and followed them to his house, a big big house in the country. They were laughing and kissing and I wanted it to be like that for me and Graham.

Ur friend who married the cop, I like her 2. The cop was knot nice to me, he kept asking questions, like I was a bad purson. I watched them. They were in love. They looked happy. Why everyone else and not me? Am I a bad purson?

U were different, u have no boyfriend, u have a carear and seam happy. I could never be a lone like you.

I found Graham in the office. He was dead. He can never hurt me again. He couldnt stay there, dead people need to go to graves.

Everything was OK until Carol came back. I did not expect Carol to get out of jail. The police say I killed him, but I didnt.

There was no white car, I lyed about that. I was scared.

Antonio, he bought weed from me and he was nice. He kissed me. I thot he loved me but his phone rang when we were together. It was his wife. He lyed to me 2. I made him help me move Graham 2 the cemtary. He did not want 2 help, but I told him I would tell his wife bout us. We used 2 play there all the time when I was a kid. There were several spots 2 get threw the fence and my brothers and I would sneak in and play hide and seek. We had a lot of fun.

 A sekurity car came down the road after we put Graham in his grave so we had to sneek out. Antoinio told me never to speek to him again, that he didn't love me.

I want someone 2 love me. Do u ever feel that way 2?

Agnes

Jennifer read the letter one more time, allowing the words to sink in, then folded it carefully and put it back into the envelope. *Agnes had suffered such loss in her struggle to love and to be loved. She didn't seem to have much self-respect, she equated being alone with loneliness and failure.*

Ryan and Sue had been sitting quietly while she read the letter. The silence in the room felt oppressive, as if the air would shatter into pieces around them if one of them spoke. Each one seemed to wait for the other to break the reverie.

Ryan spoke first, directing his question to Jennifer, "What's your take?"

"If you mean what do I think, I think Agnes had emotional problems as well as her developmental delays. Had she received support, had I known, she might not have taken her life. I think it's a tragedy. And I'm angry that she *knew* Travis and he used her too." She paused to catch her breath.

Ryan cut in. "She said Graham would never hurt her again. I took that to mean she killed him. Is that what she told you at the Falls the day she was arrested? Did she tell you she wanted to kill Antonio too?"

Jennifer looked incredulously at Ryan, then at Sue. Sue nodded in agreement.

"You read the letter?" Her voice betrayed her outrage.

293

For a second Ryan looked remorseful. He responded quickly, "It's my job."

Reeling with shock, she found her voice, "Right now my job is to get her cremated remains back to her family." Jennifer felt she could no longer stay in the room with Ryan and Sue after that revelation. The atmosphere was close and closing in on her. She needed to finish her tirade.

"This letter is about Agnes, *her* loves and *her* losses. Her life. It had my name on the envelope and the letter, not anyone else's name. No, she did not tell me she killed Graham. Antonio wasn't part of the discussion either. What makes you think I would have kept that kind of information to myself?" She shook her head, disgusted. Rising abruptly, she picked up her purse and tucked the letter inside, and turned to Sue. "Will you please walk me out?"

She stood at the door, her back to Ryan as Sue opened it, then walked down the hall ahead of Sue, her back straight and her gaze forward. As Sue unlocked the door to the lobby she didn't look at her.

"Good night," was all she said. She went to her car angrier than she'd been in a long time, even angrier than she'd been at the anonymous caller who'd tried to report a false story about her funeral home. She stopped at a drive-through, got some tea and drove to the falls. It was late afternoon, a light snow dusting the air. Jennifer walked along the parkway until she reached the place she last spoke with an unhappy Agnes. She sat on the ledge, discouraged and sad.

"Oh Agnes," she whispered. "If only you'd trusted someone enough to talk about it. But you couldn't, could you? You were so scared." She stared at the falls for a long time wondering how she could have missed the signs of Agnes' inner turmoil. Could she have helped Agnes? Probably not. It was too late now.

As the night closed in, the parkway became ablaze with the Festival of Lights. Barely noticing the bright colours, Jennifer started the long walk back to her car, her tea cold and forgotten, the night air colder.

The sun was rising before she drifted off to sleep. Ryan and Sue may have been doing their job, but she felt they were wrong to tell her so. They were wrong to think she would hide a murderer's confession, had there been one. She'd suspected that Agnes had killed Graham when she saw her measuring tape on the little table, tied in her signature knot. She was wrong. Two wrongs did not make a right and none of it negated the fact that

Agnes had taken her life. She was mostly angry with herself and her rush to judgement on Agnes's supposed guilt.

Restless and edgy, her mind rolling with convoluted thoughts, she'd slept fitfully for a few hours. She and Marcia had a busy day ahead, a new call had come in while she lay awake and she'd taken the details. She also had to return Agnes cremated remains to her mother until spring thaw, when they would have a committal service.

A phone call her broke her train of and a cheery "good morning" snapped her awake.

"Peter! How are you?"

"I'm just fine, thanks. Can you use an extra pair of hands over Christmas? I'm free."

"Absolutely. Can't wait to hear all about college. You can meet our new director at Williams and see Marcia's wedding pictures. Elaine will be so excited to see you too."

"Then I'll be in by nine. We've made the Christmas rounds with Angel's family and mine, so we'll be here in town until I have to go back to school."

"How is Angel?"

"She and the baby are doing well. The doctor

thinks it will be born early January. Angel said to say hi. I'll see you in a bit."

Feeling a bit sluggish from lack of sleep, Jennifer got out of bed, determined to maintain a positive attitude. It would be good to have Peter around for a while. She opened the funeral home and made coffee, and waited for her staff. It was a joyous reunion. After a quick coffee, Marcia and Peter left for the crematorium, while she met with the new family. The day flew by as they visited and worked together.

True to her word, Carol called that afternoon, one week after completing the renovations, to see if she could pop by to review the results and go over the final invoice. Jennifer asked if she'd mind coming early the next morning, around 8:30 a.m. because of the 11:00 a.m. funeral. She agreed.

Going downstairs early, Jennifer watched for Carol's car. When she pulled in, Jennifer noticed didn't have her usual vehicle, she was driving a brand-new Audi. Jennifer met her at the door and they did a quick tour. Everything checked out and as Jennifer signed off on the invoice, Carol unbuttoned her coat to cool off then slipped the signed invoice into the file folder as together they walked to the front door. As Elaine entered the funeral home for the day, Carol turned to greet her. Jennifer caught a flash of blue—Carol's new measuring tape tied around her neck.

Agnes wasn't the only one who knew how to tie the knot that had been around Graham's neck. Jennifer felt a flash of fear hit her. It felt as if time stood still. If Carol noticed Jennifer's reaction, she didn't show it as she put the file folder down on a chair in the lobby, buttoned her coat, and excused herself, citing another appointment. Jennifer moved quietly to the window and watched Carol pull away in her new car.

Jennifer sank into one of the chairs in the front office as Elaine hung up her coat.

"Did you see that?" Jennifer asked.

"See what?"

"Carol had a measuring tape around her neck, tied in the knot Agnes used. I've made a terrible mistake in blaming Agnes." She looked at Elaine, misery washing over her.

Elaine sat down at her desk before responding, "I did too. You know, I saw Carol on the weekend. She was with a smartly dressed man. They were looking at cars at the Audi dealership. We were stopped at a light. My first thought was that it could have been an investor for Carol's business. She kissed him, he responded, so I rather doubt he was an investor."

"Do you suppose she went back to the boyfriend, the winery owner?

"I'll look up the winery and see if there's a photo of him," Elaine said as she started searching. "I don't remember much except he was handsome and his hair was brownish in the sunlight. Ah—here it is." A little intake of breath from Elaine did not allay Jennifer's worst fears. She rose and moved around the desk.

Carol had been cleared of all charges. Her boyfriend, the winery owner, was her alibi. Elaine confirmed that the man who owned the winery was the same man who was with Carol at the dealership.

"Oh, my gosh, Elaine. Carol framed Agnes."

The two women looked at each other, horrified.

"Carol, or probably her boyfriend, strangled Graham and Carol tied that knot to implicate Agnes."

"It certainly looks that way. The police will need to be notified."

"But the police cleared her. They both had an alibi."

"Yeah, *each other*."

"I can't call Sue just because Carol can now tie the same knot as Agnes." She frowned and shook her head in disbelief.

"Call Sue, just tell her what you saw. It's up to Sue as to what happens next. I have a friend whose neighbour used Design A recently. I was telling her about the renovations and she apparently knows Carol's boyfriend. I think I'll give her a call and see what else she can tell me."

"I'll wait until you talk to her before I call Sue." Jennifer rose and went to her office, closing the door behind her. She stared at her computer screen for twenty minutes, unable to concentrate. A note on her desk from Marcia stated the Christmas call schedule needed attention. Hearing laughter in the lounge, she picked up the note and found Peter and Marcia having coffee.

"We didn't discuss the Christmas call schedule, sorry. I should have done this sooner, not two days before Christmas. I can take calls over Christmas and/or New Years. Which one would you like off Marcia?"

"New Years Eve. Ryan is off that day and we wanted to do the concert at the Falls. I can work the day before and New Years Day, if you need me."

"Naw, we can manage."

"I'll be here," Peter said. "Of course, I'd like Christmas morning off, but I'm definitely free that week and New Year's."

"Then it's settled. That was easy. You take Christmas Eve and Christmas Day off, Marcia can take New Year's." Determined to take her mind off Carol's possible role in Graham's murder, she kept the conversation light. "So Peter, tell me about college, how are your courses going? What are your fellow students like?"

"The first semester flew by. All I did was study and go to school. I made it home at least one weekend a month. I'm sorry I didn't call or pop in, I was exhausted. I really missed my family. The profs are decent and strict. I have a healthy respect for funeral service as a result. I think we'll lose a number of students over Christmas, the exams were tough and if you didn't study or take things seriously, they weren't going to pass you."

Elaine came to the door of the lounge, smiled at Peter and Marcia, and inclined her head toward Jennifer's office.

"I'll be back in a bit," Jennifer said as she followed Elaine, closing the office door behind her.

"What did you find out?"

"Apparently, if my 'gossipy' source is correct.

Carol's boyfriend's wife left him several months ago. She's in Europe with her new boyfriend. He and Carol have just started living together and he's apparently filing for divorce."

"Huh. Carol lied about breaking up with him. Maybe the police know all this."

"Or not," responded Elaine. "I wonder how many people attended Graham's funeral? Carol obviously didn't, she would've been in jail. Probably not that many. Did Agnes go?"

"I don't know, I didn't ask Brent, it didn't occur to me. Does it even make sense calling Sue and telling her Carol can tie the knot that was around Graham's neck?"

"There *is* one more thing." Carol's boyfriend is a cousin of the Larson family. His mother was the sister of the Larson patriarch you buried. My friend said she was a real beauty back in the day and the land the winery belonged to one of her lovers she apparently blackmailed."

Jennifer sat staring at her office manager, at a loss for words. "A member of the Larson family? Aylmer said I wouldn't be hearing the last of it. Are you saying Carol's boyfriend had her kill Graham to get the insurance settlement?

"They both stood to gain, Carol can now keep

the business with the insurance settlement. Maybe her boyfriend was the brains behind Graham's murder. It wouldn't surprise me if he got at least half the insurance money."

"Alymer or Elmer wanted to get back at us and tarnish the funeral home name. Does that mean Alymer or Elmer were involved in planning the murder too? Maybe they didn't call the police and try to file a complaint against the funeral home. Maybe it was Carol's boyfriend. Nothing is straightforward. It's all circumstantial." Jennifer rested her head in her hands, then sighed and looked up at Elaine, hoping she had the answer.

"I understand your reluctance to call the police but if you don't tell them, could you sleep at night wondering if Carol and her boyfriend or the Larsons did frame Agnes?"

Jennifer didn't answer, she just looked at her office manager and shook her head.

"Make the call. I'll join the others in the lounge for tea and wait." As Elaine left the office, Jennifer pulled her cell phone out and dialed Sue's number, hoping it would go to voicemail. It didn't.

"DC Ziegler."

"Hello Sue, it's Jennifer. I think you might be interested in this piece of information."

"I'm listening."

"Carol came by today, she was driving a brand-new Audi that her boyfriend bought her."

"What boyfriend?"

"The winery owner, who just happens to be a member of the *Larson* family. The ones who filed a complaint against us that the police threw out? Anyway, she didn't stay here long, she did unbutton her coat briefly and..." Jennifer took a deep breath before continuing. "Carol can tie the same knot that we thought only Agnes could do."

"Ryan did mention to me that someone called the station about your funeral home and Mr. Larson's funeral. They mentioned poor service and asked that you be investigated. The officer passed it to Ryan because he knew Marcia worked there. Ryan told the caller, who refused to identify himself, to call the Board of Funeral Services. He told the reporter the same thing when he called. I don't see a connection though. It has nothing to do with this case."

"Someone in the Larson family was trying to defame the Spencer name. I don't know who," Jennifer said miserably. "Thank goodness they didn't find out about their father's missing casket after the storm. I can't imagine what would have happened if they knew."

"We know about the car," Sue continued, glossing over Jennifer's musings. "It's in Carol's name. She bought it. Received a settlement when Graham died. Now that Carol's been cleared of all charges, the insurance company will settle. As for the knot, how do you know?"

"She had her measuring tape tied around her neck. I noticed it when she unbuttoned her coat."

"You're sure it was the same knot?"

"Positive."

"Anything else?"

"No, it was a brief visit. She was all business." She didn't tell Sue about the gossip, or Elaine seeing the two lovers together. Sue would have her own way of finding that out.

"Thanks for the information. Like I said, Carol was cleared. It's just a knot. I'm sure Carol taught Agnes or Agnes taught her how it's done. But I appreciate you bringing this to me." Then Sue deftly changed the subject. "Are you working over Christmas?"

"Yep, are you?" Jennifer had the feeling the information she'd passed on was being dismissed as insignificant. The last time she felt the police had dismissed her information, when Travis had stopped her in the hallway, it nearly cost her life. Her intuition was right then, and she was sure it was right again. *Carol killed Agnes, alibi or not. One or more of the Larson's were behind it.* Bringing herself back to the present, she forced herself to focus on Sue.

"No, I'll be working New Year's Eve, I have the week off before that. You have a Merry Christmas, if that's possible in your line of work."

"You too, if that's possible in *your* line of work" responded Jennifer, forcing herself to keep her tone light. "Bye."

As she disconnected, the landline rang. It was a first call, and she took the details and set up an appointment in an hour. The family wanted cremation and the crematorium was closed over Christmas. The service would have to be held tomorrow afternoon if the cremation was to take place before the holiday. The columbarium was open for a few days between Christmas and New Year's, they could do the cremated remains interment that week.

She tried to put Carol out of her mind. It wasn't her problem, nor was it any of her business. She had interfered enough. But the thought that Agnes might have been set up by Carol and her boyfriend, the

Larson cousin, persisted. Agnes was as much a victim as Graham. There would be no justice. *Justice delayed is justice denied. Carol got a hefty insurance settlement and is getting away with murder. The Larson's did their best to slander the funeral home and one of them is behind Graham's death. Thank goodness for David's research and squelching the story.*

But there wasn't time to dwell on it. Several more calls came in, all influenza-related deaths. Brent called, they had an overload and were sending a family to Spencer's. Flu season was escalating and with the increase in related deaths, Jennifer double-checked to ensure all the staff had their flu shots. Gordon was the only one who didn't, and he agreed to stop at the pharmacy and get it taken care of.

The next afternoon, Jennifer joined Marcia for the columbarium service, since the family had requested a limo. It was a short interment inside the new columbarium the cemetery had built. Mr. Whitney smiled politely at Jennifer as he supervised his staff member from the sidelines.

As the family and friends moved to their cars, Jennifer wished him a Merry Christmas before approaching Marcia.

"I have an errand to run, shouldn't be too long." Marcia nodded abstractly, clearly distracted by a heated conversation between several of the mourners, a married couple who were deciding who should pick up the kids at daycare. Jennifer smiled slightly at the amused expression on Marcia's face as she watched the squabble.

The winter sun was warm on her face as she walked to her car, but her heart was heavy as she thought of Agnes.

Jennifer drove to the cemetery where Mr. Larson and Doug were buried. Driving down the cemetery road she easily located Doug's grave. It wasn't hard to spot. On top of his stone were the figures he had loved, that Ronnie had carefully placed. She walked the few feet to his grave, stopping to look up at the grove of trees in the distance. Doug's grave faced his former house and property.

She looked down at the stone. Douglas James Cameron. His date of birth and death were etched in the granite, a small shovel and a tree with a tiny backhoe in the background were whimsically carved into the corner of the stone.

"Thank you," she said aloud. "Your commitment to your job cost you your life. You should have waited. You did not deserve to die. I won't forget you, and what you did for Mr. Larson and for Spencer's." Pausing, she took a minute to compose herself. "But you aren't the only that made a mistake, I did too. My mistake had grave consequences for Agnes. It'll be a long time before I forgive myself, if at all."

Jennifer walked back to her car, deep in thought. *Graham's murder may never be solved, the Larson family seems to have made sure of it with Carol's help. Sue seemed dismissive, but I have faith in her. She may yet solve this case and prove it was Carol* and *the Larson family. She has the information.*

Jennifer could hear a lone cardinal chirping somewhere in the trees as she left the cemetery to drive back to the funeral home she loved.

She had no way of knowing that the weeks ahead would test her and her staff emotionally and mentally, some past the brink of their endurance.

Thank you for reading the Spencer Funeral Home Niagara Series. If you liked the book, please rate or review it—thanks!

You can find me on:
Twitter:
@richardsonjan1
Facebook:
Janice J. Richardson
Goodreads:
https://www.goodreads.com/author/show/14979647.
Janice_J_Richardson

I would love to hear from you.

Book 4 of the Spencer Funeral Home
Niagara series

First Call

Coming late 2017

ABOUT THE AUTHOR

Jan Richardson was born in Toronto, Canada and has lived and worked in various parts of Ontario. Her original career choice was medical office assistant; her dream was to be a funeral director. Years passed, she fulfilled that dream and went to college, got her license and did a post-graduate certification.

She left funeral service to adopt and raise her special needs granddaughter, having raised a special needs daughter it was a natural progression. Her first book was non-fiction, *The Making of a Funeral Director.*

Jan currently resides in the Niagara Region. "It's is a great place to live; one never gets tired of the falls."